Cracksquatch

GARY LEE VINCENT

Burning Bulb
PUBLISHING

Cracksquatch
By **Gary Lee Vincent**

Burning Bulb Publishing
P.O. Box 4721
Bridgeport, WV 26330-4721
United States of America
www.BurningBulbPublishing.com

Cover designed by Max Cave as a work for hire between Fuzzy Monkey Films and Burning Bulb Publishing. Artwork © 2023 and used with permission of respective studios.

First Edition.

Paperback Edition ISBN: 978-1-948278-65-2

Also by Gary Lee Vincent

Novels
PASSAGEWAY
BELLY TIMBER
ATTACK OF THE MELONHEADS
WHEN THE BEDPOSTS SHAKE (RING OF THE SUCCUBUS)
IMPOUND
STRANGE FRIENDS
THE BEST ACTORS THAT EVER LIVED
THE BLIND MELODY
JEROME

Darkened—The West Virginia Vampire Series
DARKENED HILLS
DARKENED HOLLOWS
DARKENED WATERS
DARKENED SOULS
DARKENED MINDS
DARKENED DESTINIES

The Douglas River Vampire Series
RIVER: A VAMPIRE'S NIGHTMARE
ICARUS

The Crackimals Series
CRACKCOON
CRACKODILE
CRACKSQUATCH

Dedicated to
Solon Tsangaras

CHAPTER 1

"Ah, folks, don't'cha just love the clean, sweet air up here?"

The time was Friday evening. The speaker was James Gallagher, a large and muscular man who was currently leaning against a tree, way up on the slopes of Thorn Knob, and staring down into the valley leading to Teter Creek Lake. James felt it truly was a lovely afternoon up here, but then he was a man who loved the outdoors, as evidenced by his profession as a tracker. Of the opinions of his four companions, he wasn't so sure.

"Quite lovely indeed," Dr. Emily Thompson agreed, walking over to stand beside James and also gaze down into the valley.

James gave the doctor an odd sideways look. He wasn't sure what she was talking about. He had of course been referring to the air; but he suspected that the good doc, being a woman, was referring to how lovely and picturesque the view was from up here.

But anyhow, even if that was the case, he agreed with her. From up on this mountain slope, the view below was fantastic, something he often wished he could freeze and preserve, so that its purity—or rather, its already-tainted purity—could be admired forever. Despite his trying to overlook their intrusions, there was simply too much evidence of humankind in the wild scenario that lay below them.

So, James and Emily stood and enjoyed nature in their individual ways.

The three other members of their team—team leader Professor Benjamin Marshall, along with Amelia Blackwood and Jason Reynolds—lay sprawled on various bare patches of grass along their trail. Professor Marshall had called a halt in their climb so they (or rather himself) could get their breath back. At the moment tall and slender Amelia was making eyes at Jason, who was smiling politely back at her but seemed otherwise preoccupied. After Jason smiled noncommittally back at her, Amelia gave up flirting with him for the moment and turned her attention to the Professor, who was refreshing himself from a bottle of water.

"I'm not one for outdoors camping myself," she said, while nodding towards James and the doctor. "But right now, I am feeling something in the air,"

"Like what?" Professor Marshall asked her with interest, resealing his bottle and then reattaching it to his belt.

"Just *something*. It's all rather indefinable," Amelia replied in her indefinable way. "But overall, so far I'm getting a positive vibe from our being here; one that makes me feel we'll be successful in our quest for bigfoot."

Professor Marshall nodded. "I can do with some success. Our little group is long overdue to catch sight of that overgrown American ape."

Amelia laughed and then lowered her voice to a level only the professor could hear. "I don't wanna get your hopes up too much, professor, but the way I'm feeling right now, Bigfoot might be right around the corner from us."

The professor looked shocked by her statement. "Are you serious?" he asked in an equally subdued tone of voice, after a quick glance left and right to ensure that none of the others were listening in on their conversation.

Amelia nodded. "Dead serious. I can practically smell the sasquatch now. Of course, I don't mean 'smell' in a literal sense, but you know what I—"

"What you're most likely smelling is all of us, who've been sweating like racehorses 'cos of all this carrying and climbing we're doing," Jason called out, letting the two of them understand that he'd heard at least that part of their conversation. He'd been lying on his back with his hands folded over his chest, but now he leaned up on his right elbow. "I hate to say it boss, but by now we all stink."

Jason's voice was loud enough to draw the attention of both James and Emily Thompson away from their contemplation of the landscape. Both walked over towards the professor. James was laughing at Jason's comment, while, Emily, who was of a more serious temperament, was sniffing at the damp patches beneath her arm like it was a specimen in one of the Genomics Biology classes she taught at West Virginia University.

"Our sweat might be useful in attracting bigfoot to us," Emily said. There's a vein of folklore that suggests the sasquatch is attracted to human women."

Jason laughed at that. "Thank God the hairy sonofabitch ain't gay then," he said, which made Emily stare at him with a 'be serious, dude,' look.

"You're forgetting that where there are males, there are females too," the professor interjected. "Jason, those legends also speak of female sasquatches being attracted to human males."

Jason looked at James. "Is the old man pulling my leg or is he for real?"

"For real," James said. "Tho' it's equally unsubstantiated. But there are one or two stories of female sasquatches who've lost their mates abducting human males as substitutes."

Jason sudden looked worried. "So, if we're all sweating like this, and bigfoot can smell us, we're all in danger of being snatched—I mean, of never being seen again?"

"Dude, for an investigative reporter, you're a total pussy," James told him.

"Screw you, man," Jason said. "I'm just severely concerned about the state of my dick after . . . you know." Then he frowned. "How're those abducted guys gonna be able to get it up with those hairy females anyway? And then there's the size difference to consider too. Sasquatches are reputedly up to eight or ten feet in height."

"Maybe that's why there's been no survivors of the abductions to tell the tale," Amelia said. "The humongous size of the sasquatch's member rupture the women to death, while the female sasquatches are so unimpressed by human penis size that they kill their male captives out of sexual frustration."

Everyone except Emily burst out laughing at this. Emily stood watching them all, with Jason going so far as to attempt to mime the female sasquatch's sexual frustration and her accompanying rage. Then Emily decided to break it up.

"Calm down, children," she said in a cold voice. "Stop giving bigfoot a bad name. We're still searching for conclusive evidence of the creature's existence, and you're already labelling him as a slut!"

But her words had the opposite effect to what she'd intended. All she accomplished by her stern rebuke was to start everyone off laughing again.

After an additional while of staring reprovingly at her friends and companions, Emily gave up her stern attitude and joined in the laughter.

"Ah, you lot are all as bad as kids," she said, as the wind ruffled her blonde hair.

CHAPTER 2

A couple weeks ago, Dr. Emily Thompson had been reviewing student papers in her office at WVU, when her cellphone rang. After a glance at the phone's screen revealed the caller to be her good friend Benjamin Marshall, Emily had accepted the call.

"Hi, Ben, how are you?"

"Wow, Emily, you won't believe what I've got!"

The excitement she'd heard in Ben's voice had been infectious. "What is it?"

"Oh, I can't tell you about it on the phone. You'll need to come over to my house tonight."

After a moment's thought, Emily had replied. "Yeah, sure, but what is this about? Gimme a hint?"

"Cryptid business. But big. And I mean B-I-G!"

Emily immediately got it and immediately felt entranced.

"Ben, do you mean B-I-G as in bigfoot?" She'd trembled with anticipation while she awaited his reply, and had felt almost orgasmic when he'd replied in the affirmative.

"I sure do, girl. I sure do. This time it looks like we've got ourselves a winner!"

Ben Marshall wasn't usually this effusive. Which meant that whatever he'd discovered had to be really hot; not something to be sniffed at.

That night Emily Thompson had attended a meeting at Benjamin Marshall's house.

On arriving there, she hadn't been surprised to discover she wasn't the only guest. Or that she knew the other people there. Such had been the excitement and barely-concealed anticipation in Ben's voice over the phone that she could already tell that her friend and mentor had stumbled onto something big.

***

Benjamin and Emily went back a long way; the pair had known each other and worked together in some capacity for almost a decade and a half. At the moment, both of them lectured at WVU's Life Sciences Building.

Ben was a professor in the university's Humanities and Social Sciences department. Ben was in his mid-fifties, the stereotypical balding professor with a beer bulge, while Emily was in her late thirties, the stereotypical academic spinster just verging on a lonely and miserable middle age. She was an attractive enough blonde, but relationships just never seemed to jell for her.

A good number of her colleagues and family thought she was a closet lesbian, but such wasn't the case. Just as with lots of other career women, Dr. Emily Thompson had simply never found the right man for her; or maybe she had, but had been too distracted at the time by her academic interests to recognize the value of what she had until she no longer possessed it.

***

The other attendees at the meeting in Ben Marshall's house that night were Jason Reynolds, Amelia Blackwood and Ben's cousin James Gallagher. Amelia and Jason were in their mid-thirties; James in his late-forties. The men were all drinking beers, but a bottle of white wine had been opened up on the coffee table for Amelia.

By way of profession, Jason was an investigative reporter, Amelia a psychic, and James a professional tracker and woodsman (the whole Marshall/Gallagher family having originated in the mountainous woodlands of Randolph County, West Virginia).

Diverse people indeed they were, with (exception in Ben and Emily's case) even more diverse professions. What however drew these five people together, what had both created and unified this little group of theirs to the point that it had existed now for six years, was their shared love of cryptid science and lore, most importantly, their belief in the existence of bigfoot.

To similar but still varying degrees, Ben Marshall, Emily Thompson, James Gallagher, Amelia Blackwood and Jason Reynolds were obsessed with bigfoot.

All five of them were members of the Bigfoot Field Researchers Organization (BFRO), and regularly went on BFRO expeditions.

Outside of their work and family, such research into the possibility that the legends were true, extended for these five beyond the bounds at which it could be described as a mere hobby. In their case, the search for cryptids could accurately be described as an obsession.

There could be no doubt at all that all those present in the professor's living room that fateful night were totally committed to validating that sasquatch was, indeed, real.

***

The meeting had been held Professor Marshall's living room, which was a shrine to his interest in those creatures—monsters and myths—that were supposed to exist just beyond the glimpse of human eyes.

Professor Marshall had copies of all the classic bigfoot recordings, both audio and video, including the famed Patterson–Gimlin film. His walls were hung with stills from multiple sasquatch films, and huge pictures of sasquatch footprints. He had several large glass-walled cabinets set in the corners of both his living room and study, each of which housed plaster casts of bigfoot feet, along with realistic latex replicas of those same feet. One of the glass cabinets even contained some of the original wood carvings of sasquatch feet allegedly used by Ray Wallace to fake bigfoot footprints in 1958 in Humboldt County, California.

The professor's bookcases were stuffed with volumes on cryptids and other biological curiosities, including documentation on alien abductions and such.

His entire residence had the atmosphere of a museum to it—a museum to missing things, with himself—complete with graying hair and bald spot—fulfilling the role of museum curator, the guardian entrusted with protecting the knowledge of suspected, but never fully proven creatures.

Professor Marshall was able to indulge his obsession in this way because he lived alone, his wife having left him a decade ago for a younger and 'less unrealistic' man. Marie had never shared her husband's obsession with bigfoot, dismissing it as 'unprofitable nonsense.'

***

As far as I'm concerned, Emily had thought that night while Ben poured her a glass of wine, *Ben and Marie's non-amicable divorce was all for the best. Now that Marie is gone, Ben can be as obsessed with Marie's 'unprofitable nonsense' as he likes, which is as much as I like too.* Then she'd sighed. *Oh, it's just too bad that I'm not the marrying kind. If I was, it would be a dream to be Ben's wife—we have so much in common!*

Professor Marshall had handed Emily her glass with a smile. He had a very soft spot for Emily, one that bordered on romantic feeling.

"Alright, dear friends, I know you'll be wondering why I invited you all over here at such short notice and in such a state of excitement," the professor had said afterward.

There had been nods all around and grunts from both James and Jason. The men were seated in chairs on either side of Marshall's electric fireplace, while the women sat on either end of the professor's tattered sofa, concessions to luxury having departed from his life at the same time his ex-wife Marie had. The space Emily and Amelia had left in the middle of the sofa was intentional, so Marshall could sit there once he was done with the pacing he was currently engaged in.

Consciously or unconsciously, everyone had arranged themselves around an idling laptop that sat on the coffee table. A digital camera sat beside the laptop, but wasn't connected to it.

"Okay," Professor Marshall had said, coming to a halt between the laptop and the space the ladies had reserved for him on the couch. "I think we've found the motherlode. I mean *the real* freaking sasquatch motherlode."

Everyone had leaned forward to hear what he had to say next. To their surprise, Professor Marshall had gestured to James Gallagher and then sat down.

James hadn't gotten to his feet. He'd just gestured at the laptop with his beer and then put the beer to his mouth and took a long pull from the can before speaking:

"Well, last week, while searching for a missing camper up in the Laurel Mountain area—you know, the steep range that runs above the Sleepaway Campground—I found THAT digital camera," he said gesturing, "that's now lying there on the coffee table, abandoned in the grass. It's a recent model of Canon DSLR, and clearly hadn't been abandoned for too long . . ."

"How'd you tell that?" Amelia had enquired. "What I mean is, how could you possibly know how long it's been abandoned for? Since like you said, it was just lying there in the grass."

"I was just coming to that," James had replied, then picked up his beer and took another long pull, one that apparently emptied the can, because he gave his cousin an inquiring look that made Ben get to his feet and head towards the kitchen, with Jason calling out after him, "And another beer for me too, man!"

Emily had thought she'd noticed something weird about Jason's behavior that night; he'd seemed all edgy-like. But after his comment about also needing more beer, they'd all returned their attention to what James was saying.

"Well, for one thing, the camera was squeaky clean," James explained with his gaze on Amelia. "And also, it wasn't rusted or muddy, like you'd expect if it had been rained on a lot. Anyway, that was my initial impression on picking it up. Yeah, and it also still had some battery power in it—maybe about a quarter charge. So I turned it on and had a look at the footage."

"I'll take over the explanation from this point," Professor Marshall had said then, returning to the room with three beers, one of which he kept for himself after handing the others to James and Jason.

"So, James watched the last footage shot on the recovered camera," the professor had gone on. "His original intention was to hand the device in at the nearby ranger station, in case a camper had mislaid it and later came looking back for it. But while watching the footage, he recognized the person being filmed. So, he delayed handing in the camera and brought it over to me instead."

"So, who was it?" Jason had asked with a news reporter's bluntness.

"Patience, man," Marshall had replied. "James and I are going to let you three watch the video recording for yourselves and see what you think."

That said, Marshall had bent over the laptop and tapped the screen on. Once it came to life, he'd double-clicked on a video file. "We transferred everything on the camera over for safekeeping and wiped the memory card clean. All that's on it now are some boring home movies. But even with that cleanup job, once you've watched the footage you'll all agree that there's no point handing the camera in at the ranger station."

The movie on the laptop was already playing when Professor Marshall took his seat on the couch. James had remained in his seat, but Jason had moved over to sit on the couch also, pushing Amelia inward.

The first thing they'd seen was a shot of the forest. Semi-dark woods and the time seemed to be early evening. They'd heard the sounds of grass rustling, leaves moving, and also twigs snapping underfoot. The hand that held the camera was steady and spoke of the cameraperson's experience. The person filming wasn't walking on a proper forest trail.

For a short period of time this was all that happened, just the sound of two or more people walking, while the camera panned up and down and zoomed back and forth between the trees.

Then a voice said, "Hey, Donnie, wait there. Let's film here."

The camera obediently swiveled and after a short delay, focused on a young woman; pretty with curly brunette hair.

Seeing the woman had triggered a sharp intake of breath from Jason and the two women sitting on the couch.

"Hey, that's Bonnie B. Wilde!" Emily had said in surprise.

"It certainly *is* her," Amelia had instantly agreed in equal surprise.

***

Bonnie B. Wilde was a cryptid researcher and YouTuber who'd gone missing the previous month. She and her boyfriend/cameraman Donald Duval had been teasing a 'huge exclusive cryptid scoop' for weeks, but had been completely hush-hush as to what it was they had discovered and were gearing up to reveal to the world.

"Hey, guys!" Bonnie B. Wilde said, with a bright wave at the camera. "As you all can see, Donnie and me are about keeping our promise to you all to bring you the cryptid scoop of the year."

"Not the year, baby; of the damn century," Donnie's voice said off camera.

Bonnie frowned at her off-screen boyfriend and then nodded. "Yeah, that's right. This is the cryptid scoop of the fucking century. And do you know why this is so, people? It's because . . . wait for it everyone—it's because we've found bigfoot!" Bonnie's eyes were gleaming so brightly that she might've been high on drugs while the video was recorded.

"Somebody correct me if I'm wrong," Amelia had said, "but that young woman is as high as a kite."

"Nah, she's just overly excited," Jason had said.

"Shush!" Emily had said. "I don't wanna miss any of this."

"Now here's the real weird thing about this," Bonnie was saying. "Apparently, like we've all suspected for all of these years, bigfoot lives right around the corner from us. Up here on . . ." Then she giggled coyly. "But no, I'm not gonna tell you where we currently are, 'cos if I do, you're all going to come visit; and then you'll scare bigfoot away and we won't know where to find him anymore." Then there was a pause during which Bonnie got out her powder compact and checked her looks, then touched up her red lipstick.

"I don't see what's so unusual about this," Jason had said without thinking. "As far as I can tell, it's just more of Bonnie B. being her usual fake, annoying self. Then he'd reconsidered and apologized. "Oh, sorry, guys. I get it—this is the found footage of how she and Donald went missing?"

"Keep watching, dude," James had said, giving Jason an odd look. "And please, lay off the fucking beers till we're done here?"

Jason had laughed. "Dude, you're right. I'm losing track of things rather quickly tonight." That said, he'd turned to their host. "Okay if I use your bathroom, man? The beers already seem tired of my bladder."

"Be my guest," Marshall had replied, with a vague gesture towards the hallway. "You know the way." But once Jason had departed for the bathroom, Marshall too had stared after him for a short while with a thoughtful look on his face.

So Jason had departed, just when Bonnie B. decided she was pretty enough for the microphone again. Donnie had kept filming her in the interim, so there was no break in the movie.

"And so, without letting on the secret of exactly where bigfoot lives, we're on our way to go visit him," Bonnie said, posing for the camera. "Now, I know what you're all thinking now—that Donnie and I are gonna be faking all of this, and plan to have a laugh at the expense of everyone here, but I assure you that we really did get a lead to—hey, what's that?"

Bonnie's expression had changed so suddenly that everyone— including both Professor Marshall and James, who'd watched the tape before—had started back in their seats. It was at this point that the mood in the professor's living room had altered. Before this, both Emily and Amelia's anticipation had been tempered with the knowledge that they were searching for the impossible and it was too much to hope for to actually stumble on it.

But the way Bonnie B. Wilde's facial expression had suddenly altered left no doubt in both women's minds that Bonnie had seen something unusual. Everyone knew Bonnie. She was passably genuine; as genuine as anyone who spent their life chasing shadows could be. Bonnie was no actress; the few times she and Donnie had attempted to fake a cryptid prank, it had been corniest thing anyone had ever seen.

But now, all of a sudden, Bonnie's jaw was hanging open, and her eyes were staring off-screen like those of a believer in aliens watching a spaceship land.

Of course, the pretty cryptid hunter might just have been on narcotics, but no one watching really believed that.

"Why are you looking like that?" Donnie was asking, prompting Bonnie to speechlessly jab her finger in the direction her gaze was riveted.

Donnie swung the camera around to see what Bonnie was seeing, but somehow, he never completed the turn. There was a sudden blur of motion and the camera visual skewed in a crazy angle like it had been knocked out of Donnie's hands.

"What the hell is happening?" Jason had asked, returning from the bathroom at that point in the film viewing.

But no one had replied him. Maybe only James, who'd had less of a vantage-point view of the laptop than the others, had heard the question; even Professor Marshall had his attention riveted to the screen.

Jason had shrugged, sat down on the far right edge of Marshall's couch again, and tried to figure out what was going on. After a few seconds, the distorted onscreen action once more resolved into a sequence of images that were easy to follow.

The first thing they saw was Donnie hitting the floor a few feet away from the camera, which was now lying on the ground, with its lens aimed sideways through the grass. Donnie had hit the ground on his back. He had a pained look on his face, and it was impossible to tell if he was dead or alive.

For about thirty seconds, he lay there like that, with his eyes closed. This was in tandem with a lot of feminine screaming, loud and low-pitched primal grunting like the noise a gorilla makes, and Bonnie yelling, "Put me down! Put me down!" and "Don't you dare touch me there!" There were also some rather obscene slurping noises which prompted a plea of, "Damnit, stop licking me!"

All of this took place off-camera, so no one could see what was really happening to the famous YouTuber and cryptid investigator. But then Donnie opened his eyes and reached out for the camera. His eyes were glazed, and he both looked stunned and was bleeding from a cut above the hairline, but, operating purely on instinct born from years of being a cameraman, he picked up the camera. This action was followed by a few seconds of further confused visuals, while Donnie again got the camera in focus; and then everyone was treated to the sight of a half-naked Bonnie B. Wilde weeping profusely, while a huge amount of a gluey substance dripped down her chest and belly.

"Nice rack!" Jason had approved, but once again, no one paid him the slightest attention, because the next moment, something huge, dark, and hairy (but undefined now that night was falling), grabbed hold of Bonnie and carried her off.

There was no mistaking what had hold of Bonnie B. Wilde. It was a sasquatch, bigfoot in person. The creature had to be at least eight feet tall, way too tall for Bonnie and Donnie to have hired one of their basketball player friends to fake in a monkey suit. Bigfoot had Bonnie up in the air in something like a fireman's carry, and as it bore her away between the trees and up the mountainside, she was beating on its back with her fists, while her breasts bobbed teasingly up and down, and while yelling angrily at her boyfriend:

"Help me, Donnie, you sonofabitch! Save me, you spineless coward! HELP ME SOMEBODY!"

For a few seconds it looked like Donnie would indeed attempt a rescue. This impression was created by the camera following Bonnie and bigfoot closely. But then the imagery went topsy-turvy all of a sudden and then there was just noise, and the sound of breaking branches. The camera rolled to a halt and remained focused on an image of darkening grass.

"James thinks at that point he tripped and rolled downhill," Professor Marshall had said afterwards. "Kid probably drowned in the river, but at a far enough distance from the Sleepaway Campground that no one's noticed his body yet. And if he washed up on the river bank and the animals got to his corpse . . . I doubt there'll be much left of him for his family to ID."

His words had created a horrible mental picture in the watchers' amazed minds, and no one was willing to comment on them.

By that point, the tension in the room had become as taut as a bowstring that was ready to snap. But by slow stages, it finally lessened to the point where Professor Marshall asked his companions:

"So, now that you've watched it, what do you think? Real or faked?"

"Oh, it's real alright," Emily had immediately said in a shocked voice. "I see no sign of fakery in what we just watched."

"Yeah," Amelia quickly agreed. "It has a genuine vibe to it."

James had nodded. "Even if the sasquatch could be faked, and I don't see how it could, from what we know of her, Bonnie B. is too much of a lady to ever show her boobs in public."

"Or let herself get splattered with bigfoot cum like that," Jason had drily commented. "That stuff looked like someone emptied several jars of mayonnaise on the girl."

"I suppose bigfoot was sexually frustrated," Amelia had joked, with a sly wink at Jason.

Jason had grinned back at her, much more alive and present now since his short trip to the bathroom.

Professor Marshall had once more got to his feet. After circling the coffee table to a point directly in front of the electric fireplace, he'd faced his semicircle of friends with his hands in his pockets.

"Well, now we all know exactly what happened to Bonnie B. Wilde. Why she's not been either seen or heard from for about a month. Like all the rest of you, James and I were both at first suspicious when we heard Miss Wilde and Donald had gone missing. It seemed just another prank the pair of them would pull . . ."

"Yeah, like that damn flying saucer April Fool's Day prank of theirs . . ." Emily had said. I felt like killing the bitch after they did that one."

Professor Marshall had nodded back at her. "We all did, Emily. Oh, we all did. But since they apologized . . ." He'd frowned. "But let's not get sidetracked here. What I was going to say is, they went missing and no one's heard from either of them for a month."

"After we found the tape, the professor had me run some research on the pair," James Gallagher had said. "Just routine detective work, checking the facts of their disappearance."

Jason had stared at Marshall in surprise. "Why not ask me to do it? It's part of what I do for a living."

"Yes it is," the professor had readily agreed. "But in this case, there seemed no point in troubling you. All I asked James to find out were the basics of the case."

"Same thing," Jason had replied. Then he'd shrugged. "So what did James find out anyway?"

James had shrugged too. "First of all, Bonnie and Donnie hadn't been seen at home either. The neighbor of theirs that I spoke to said she'd not seen them in over two weeks . And normally she and Bonnie chatted several times a week. No phone contact either. Nothing. I asked her if the cops had called; she said she wasn't sure they had. More revealing, however, Bonnie's red Camry was parked outside their house. I ran a finger over it, finger came away black with dust. So they definitely weren't home."

"It was only when James had completed his investigation, that I called you all in for a meeting," the professor had said afterwards.

"I'm feeling a little weird about all this," Emily had said then, with a worried look on her face. "Maybe calling *us* wasn't the right idea. Maybe you and James should have given the camera and the recording to the police immediately after watching it. From the look of things, Bonnie's life may be in danger. The police and forest rangers are better equipped to rescue her from . . ."

"From bigfoot?" Marshall had laughed. "Be reasonable, Emily. We take this recording to the cops and they'll throw us out of the station. A cryptid-obsessed YouTuber kidnapped by bigfoot? You know as well as I do that the cops are gonna send us straight to the *National Enquirer.*"

Emily had sighed at his reply, because she knew he was right; the police would simply laugh them out of the station; after they'd had their fill of ogling Bonnie's breasts of course.

Instead of commenting further, Emily had leaned forward and refilled her wineglass from the bottle beside Marshall's laptop. An image had remained frozen in her mind: Bonnie's terrified (and also enraged) face as she was helplessly carried off, with tears of embarrassment (but also rage) in her eyes as she reached out her hands to her stunned boyfriend for help.

"I'm uneasy about this too," Amelia had said. "As far as we can tell, Bonnie's still out there. And she needs our help."

"Hey, the sasquatch only jerked off on her, he didn't try to fuck her or eat her," James had said.

"Doesn't mean he won't try to fuck or eat her once she's back in his cave," Amelia had retorted. "Don't be so callous."

"Just saying. From the rumors, bigfoot is so well hung he'd never get his monster dick up inside a human woman away."

"I wouldn't be so sure of that," Professor Marshall had disagreed. "Remember, James, some women copulate with horses and donkeys, and even claim they get sexual pleasure from such mismatched congress. It's unlikely bigfoot will be much larger than those animals."

Emily had sighed. "Well, Ben, we'll never know until we find him, will we?" She stood up and looked around the room, then pointed to the laptop and said, "Alright, everyone, so that we don't keep debating the size of bigfoot's penis and what it might do to Bonnie B. Wilde, let's take a vote. Everyone in favor of our going to look for bigfoot at the mountain where Bonnie disappeared, raise your hand."

That night, the vote went exactly as Emily had expected. Everyone had raised their hands. Each face had been imprinted with the same interest in retracing Bonnie and Donnie's footsteps and searching for the sasquatch that they now realized was nearby, and which was possibly theirs, if not for the taking, at least for the filming.

After that, it had simply been a matter of planning and waiting for the right weekend, when everyone had nothing else already planned that they couldn't get out of.

CHAPTER 3

Back in the here and now, Jason walked along behind the rest of the team. Being the one responsible for documenting their trip and what they found, he had a handheld video camera with him, but for the moment wasn't recording anything because, for the moment at least, nothing interesting was happening.

No matter what James and Amelia say 'bout how gorgeous the view is from up here, the professor isn't gonna want to review hours of footage of the countryside, like Donnie filmed with Bonnie. Best I just keep my recordings short and sweet and to the point. That way I'll be saving hard drive space too.

Jason had recorded some footage at the beginning of their expedition, when they'd parked their expedition vehicle, the professor's white RV, in the north parking lot, which was situated at a slightly lower level of Laurel Mountain, but which was the highest access point by road. The footage had consisted of everyone on the expedition introducing themselves, and the professor explaining why they were all here and what they hoped to accomplish by this 'daring trip' up the mountainside.

Professor Marshall had said the recording was important, because if they did find bigfoot, they would make a video of the encounter for the world to watch.

Yeah, the professor's right. If we do find bigfoot, filming everyone's introductions afterwards will make it impossible to capture the original excitement we all felt on our arrival here.

So for the moment, loaded up with both backpack and bags of stuff, Jason trudged along with the others, with his camera dangling in his left hand, ready for use at a moment's notice.

Even so, Jason might have recorded some footage had he been feeling better. But right now he felt shaky. The drug jones was on him and his insides felt all tangled up on themselves.

The problem was that, so far during their long climb since daybreak, he'd not been able to sneak away from their little group to 'crack up.' All he'd been able to do today was chew the rock, which greatly lessened the high. He tapped his left trouser pocket, and felt a slight relief. Yes, the package was still there. His backup supply was a much larger package that he'd left back in the professor's camper.

Well, it was time he fixed himself up. He already felt shaky from withdrawal, and doubted it would be long before the others also noticed that he wasn't himself.

At that thought, Jason laughed. *Fuck it, I've not been myself since the evil day that I first tried Agent Orange.*

Their group was currently arranged with the professor and James in the lead, Amelia and Jason in the middle, and Emily bringing up the rear. Everyone was loaded up with backpacks and research and camping gear. Emily and James were also rolling wheeled equipment cases behind them.

As far as Jason was concerned, this arrangement wouldn't do at all. Jason had a pocket full of the new designer crack cocaine named Agent Orange, and even though he could simply pull out one of the little orange nuggets and pop it in his mouth, doing so would certainly lead to the women asking him what he was eating, and then asking him to share it with them.

Oh no, ladies, you definitely don't want this stuff. I don't even want it myself, but either it's impossible to kick an Agent Orange habit, or I'm simply not the man to do it.

So Jason pretended to stumble, then he grabbed his left foot.

Amelia chose that moment to smile at him. "Are you okay?" she asked in concern.

Jason forced a smile back at her. "My shoelaces came untied. You guys go on; I'll double up to catch up with you." He prayed desperately, that she wouldn't insist on waiting till he'd done up the undone shoelace, or noticed that it hadn't come undone at all. That would be disastrous to Jason's plans. Because now, the craving seemed to be growing stronger by the minute.

He was relieved when Amelia just nodded and resumed walking, stopping to speak to Emily Thompson about something. Jason watched Amelia's ass bounce in her pants and grimaced.

knew Amelia wanted him, and she was his type of woman too. Later maybe, they might hook up. But at the moment the drug craving was on him and he had no interest in anything else.

Once certain that no one was peeking back at him and that even if they were, he was too far away for them to see what he was doing, Jason quickly reached into his pocket and fished out the packet of Agent Orange. To better keep his secret, he'd stashed the drug in an empty SNUS can.

Fuck, I really shouldn't be doing this. This shit is fucking gonna kill me if I keep it up.

But hate it as much as he liked, he was already an addict, and his self-recrimination and good sense were no match for his craving.

After a further glance ahead, and a look down at the Sleepaway Campground that was now clearly visible through a break in the hillside trees, Jason got out one of the little orange chunks of the drug.

Just staring at it entranced him. To the uninitiated it really did look like regular candy—say a mini-sized orange marshmallow, even down to the whitish dusting of powder coating it. But that was as far as its innocence went.

Agent Orange did something to you—it really did; but then all crack cocaine affected one that way. It was just that Agent Orange somehow dug deeper into the human psyche, and so pulled one deeper into the cycle of addiction than normal crack did; which of course resulted in both a more harrowing comedown from the superlative high that the drug provided its users, and also more destruction of the individual's life.

Still, Jason put one of the orange chunks on his tongue. After savoring its bitter, non-candy taste for a few seconds, he gave into the urge to bite into it. While chewing it, he mused on the fact that doing so lessened the high he could be getting if he was using a crack pipe. But once again, he realized that in the outdoors like this, up here in the mountains, that couldn't be helped.

But just to make certain he felt stable enough for the rest of the day, or at least till they all set up camp, Jason ate another of the orange 'marshmallows.'

Then without waiting for the drug to kick in, he hurried along the faint forest trail after his friends.

CHAPTER 4

The time was mid Friday evening and forest ranger Gary Bentley was just winding up his tour of the hiking trails around the Sleepaway Campground.

While making his way east toward the campground's main parking lot, Gary checked his watch. *Alright, just a brief walk along the cabins across the river and I'll be leavin' for home. Damn if it ain't been a long day.*

The reason Gary felt today's shift had been longer than usual was that he'd spent the first half of it lecturing obtuse campers on the need to stop littering the campground. The older and more experienced campers hadn't been the problem. They usually weren't. The young ones—college kids and yuppie couples—those were Gary's littering headache.

I guess they don't teach 'em smarts in high school or business school, Gary thought sourly as he made the sharp right turn in the trail that led down to the river bridge. *It should be common sense really; don't throw your damned beer cans wherever you see fit. We've got trash cans around the campground for that kinda thing. Take care of the forest and it'll take care of you. That's just simple logic.*

Gary loved the forest and the open countryside. He'd loved the wild and its wildlife all of his life, and now that he'd followed in his father's footsteps and was tasked with preserving nature and keeping an eye on the forests, he didn't like encountering those who figured the woods were simply a houseless version of the city.

His simmering thoughts cooled as he headed for the river. After a while he smiled. *Maybe I'm just getting old, and can't really recall how things were when Charlotte and I were young folk too. I guess once you've been partying it up a little hard, all the drugs you've been taking would make throwing beer cans in the damn river seem logical too.*

Gary's amused thoughts died when he reached a certain rocky ledge a short distance from the bridge he was headed for. The sight of the ledge brought back terrible memories.

For the first time in a long while Gary Bentley found himself thinking about Agent Orange.

Agent Orange: the orange-colored variant of crack cocaine that a mad-genius scientist by the name of Max Carillo had created.

Agent Orange—named after the Vietnam War defoliating agent—gave its users the ultimate high, but at the twin price of both an accelerated breakdown of the user's sanity, coupled with the simultaneous development of a frightening tendency towards unprovoked violence.

An Agent Orange junkie needed no trigger to commit the most heinous of murders. FBI scientists had now worked out that the drug systematically altered human brain chemistry, rewiring it to something alien and primal.

Yes, Agent Orange was real bad stuff. And that was before one took into consideration that the most hardcore users wound up with bright orange eyes.

Max was dead now, but his formula lived on. Now, however, that the dangers of Agent Orange had been publicized, only the most desperate thrill seekers tended to patronize its dealers.

Gary stood by the river and mused on what had happened here in the past. Then he looked aside, peering through the trees at a nearby stretch of forest floor that barely a month ago had been strewn with horribly mutilated corpses from the rampage of an Agent-Orange-addicted Nile crocodile. The orange crack variant had driven the huge beast out of its mind, and sent it on a killing spree all the way down to Teter Creek Lake.

Thinking back on that, Gary heaved a sigh of relief. He hadn't caught wind of an Agent-Orange-related death in a month, which was much different from when Max was running his crack laboratory in the trailer park down by Teter Creek.

To Gary's mind, Agent Orange was simply another party drug. His real problem with it had nothing to do with humans using it.

We've got free will; we can blow out our brains if we so choose. No, my beef with that evil stuff is what it does to animals; like what happened with Elvis.

Elvis had been one of his wife Charlotte's tame raccoons. Somehow Elvis had gotten hooked on Agent Orange and then . . .

Gary sighed. *The only reason Elvis didn't do as much harm as the crocodile did was because he was smaller in size than the damn croc. The hell crap am I thinkin'? I think the little SOB did even more damage than the crocodile. Well, thank heavens that's over now. Maybe Agent Orange isn't gone for good; but so long as it stays out of these here woods, that's fine with me.*

Managing an optimistic smile, Gary stepped past the rocky ledge, descended to the river and climbed the bridge.

CHAPTER 5

After a while of walking, James called a halt. It wasn't night yet, but the overlapping layers of forest around and above them made it seem later in the evening than it was.

"Okay, folks, I'd say that right about here is where our young friend Bonnie got abducted. Meaning," he added as the rest of them gathered around him," that we need to be extra-careful from here on. Bigfoot could be just around the corner from where we are."

But Professor Marshall shook his head. "No, no, James," he said with some amusement. "You're forgetting that bigfoot is naturally shy of us humans. His usual behavior is to avoid us—like we're the plague, I could say."

But Amelia quickly disagreed with him: "I think I agree with James on this one, professor. In that video that James found, bigfoot seemed anything but shy to me."

"Well, maybe the big guy was camera-shy," Jason joked.

But really Jason's mind wasn't on what he was saying. While apparently present there in the forest with the others, Jason Reynolds was fighting a private war, one that he'd begun himself when he'd fallen back from their group to dope himself with Agent Orange.

A major problem with Agent Orange, and one that Jason was personally familiar with, was that it made its users ultra-violent.

At the moment Amelia was laughing at what Jason had just said about bigfoot being camera shy, and her amusement made him feel like killing her. Even while smiling at the others, his mind was seething with rage—he wanted to slam his video camera into Amelia's pretty face until her happy expression imploded into a bloody mess. No, that would be too quick a death; he wanted to strangle her instead, wrap his hands around her delicate throat and grin at her while she asphyxiated. No, no, no, not his hands; the best way to kill Amelia would be to strangle her with the strap of his camera—slip it around her neck and tighten it slowly . . . very slowly, so that her face turned blue . . . until . . . until . . .

Jason fought against the evil desire coursing through him, till he imagined his mind would explode from the unrelieved urge to violence. To help himself he looked from Amelia to Emily, but it was the same; a cloud of red rage—no, orange rage—flooded his brain like a spilled soft drink. In desperation, with his brain seemingly close to shutdown, he turned to stare at the professor instead.

"Hey, are you okay?" Professor Marshall asked Jason.

"I'm . . . I'm okay, man," Jason said, shoving away Marshall's friendly arm. "I just feel a little under the weather. It's this heat, I think." After making that comment, he realized he'd slipped up. There was no heat today, none except for the heated emotions that now raged inside of him. In addition, they'd paused beneath a covering of trees that effective blocked off the sun and its rays.

"Heat?" Emily asked in clear surprise, tossing her long blonde hair to the side to see him better. "Are you getting a fever?"

"Look, I'm okay," Jason growled in misery, as the urge to leap on Emily and beat her black and blue almost overcame him.

Emily continued looking at him like she didn't believe him, which only made Jason madder. "Let's just get on with the damn search for bigfoot," he managed to say, in a normal tone of voice. "I'll be fine. If it's not the weather affecting me, then maybe it was something I had for lunch."

Professor Marshall looked unsure, but then nodded. "Okay, if you say so. But you really don't look too good."

Jason forced a smile he hoped looked convincing. "I'm be fine. Please, professor, go on with what you were saying about bigfoot."

Marshall nodded and turned his attention back to the others. "Alright. Now we know for sure that bigfoot was here. So, I'd say this is a great place to set up our camp. What d'you think, James?"

James nodded. "It's as good as any." The muscular and experienced tracker (who was also laden with twice as much camping gear as the others) gestured around the shadowy glade they stood in. "For one thing, we've lots of cover from view of the campers below, but also lots of space to camp in, so bigfoot won't be able to surprise us."

"We need to stay together," Emily said. "All sleep in the same tent if possible."

Jason laughed. "Seriously, Emily? That just occurred to you?"

She nodded, a worried frown on her face. "Yes, yes, I'm serious. I was fine with everything up until we got here. But now that we're actually doing it . . . I don't know how I feel anymore."

Amelia laughed loudly. "Emily, I never figured you for a drama queen. You're acting like this is your first dance in the woods."

Emily sighed and looked confused. "I know, I know. But . . . I can't stop seeing Bonnie's B. Wilde's face as she was borne away, never to be seen again."

"Well it's too late for regrets now," Professor Marshall told her. "We're setting up camp here. You girls will be sharing as usual; as will us guys. But, since you're really worried about this, I'll make the concession of us setting up the tents closer together than usual."

"That'll make me feel safer," Emily said.

Professor Marshall looked around for James, but the tracker was already marking off the camp boundaries, by drawing a line along the ground with a sharp stick. James looked around, saw the professor staring at him, and gestured him over, saying, "Hey, we've gotta set up all these motion sensors before it grows too dark."

The motion sensors were designed to emit a signal when something living passed them, with the idea being that if a sasquatch entered the camp at night, its presence would activate the units, which would then both rouse the camp, and also trigger several night-vision-enabled cameras placed in the surrounding trees, which would then make both video and still-image recordings of the legendary hairy recluse.

Of course, seeing as such nighttime intruders into their camp could include rodents, deer and even bears, the motion sensors could be set to discriminate based on the animals' size, which also prevented them going off each time one of the campers stepped out to relieve themselves. The sensors were current on their 'Giant' setting.

Jason watched the professor and his tracker cousin place sensors near a couple of trees, and then walked over to help Amelia unpack and erect the inflatable tent that she and Emily would be sleeping in

"You know, I've been interested in bigfoot since I was this high," Amelia said when Jason joined her, while with a flat, horizontal palm indicating a height around her waist." She laughed. "That must've been when I was around six years old."

Jason started the pump to inflate the tent and he let her talk.

Either by genetics or by personal training, Amelia Blackwood had a very pleasing voice. At the moment, it was to him a calming influence, something he felt desperately in need of. He still felt the violent urges, but for now at least, their grip on his brain had lessened. It occurred to Jason that he'd attempt to go cold turkey on Agent Orange tonight.

"So, yeah," Amelia continued, "it was definitely around then, when I was about six or seven years of age, that I became aware of bigfoot's existence. He appealed to me as this creature who was living free of parental control, who could do whatever he wanted, and yet had no parents reprimanding him for not tidying up his toys or eating his vegetables."

Jason laughed. "Trust me, I know how you felt."

"Of course, there's also the fact that back then I desperately wanted a dog, but my dad said I was too scatterbrained to take care of one; and, viewed in a particular kiddy way, bigfoot has a 'doggy' kind of look to him." She nodded at Jason. "Was it the same with you?"

"Oh yeah, it was very similar. I didn't so much want a dog as I wanted a Chewbacca of my own to ride with in the Millennium Falcon, and you gotta admit that bigfoot has serious 'wookie-appeal.' So, I've been looking for the big guy since then. Like just to walk up to him and say 'hi, man, how's life up there in the Milky Way?' "

That cracked them both up, and also made Emily look their way. Emily was sitting cross-legged on the grass with a laptop on her lap and was inputting figures into it. Her face as she watched them was as serious as ever; but then Emily hardly ever laughed. Jason felt it was part of the reasons why, as pretty as Emily was, she couldn't keep a man interested in her.

What Emily was doing with the laptop was programming a green box on the ground beside her that analyzed the pheromone content of the air. The box, which she nicknamed "Sniffy," was designed to detect trace amounts of odoriferous animal skin secretions, and it was supposed to let them know where bigfoot had been, with the idea being that by analyzing the air in this way, the box would lead them to their quarry.

If bigfoot won't come to the seeker, then the seeker will go to bigfoot. By any fucking means necessary.

There were other devices that would be called into play sooner or later during their search; but none of these concerned either Jason or Amelia. The two of them left the technical details to the two academics and James.

I'm just here to record everything, Jason thought, as the inflating tent stopped looking like a deflating balloon and more like a human residence. *This is gonna be monumental and I gotta ensure everything is caught on camera. And Amelia? well, Amelia's here to sort-of guide us. Not that I'm convinced she can in this case. We aren't ghost-hunting or anything like that.*

Amelia made her living as a psychic. Jason wasn't sure if she really could connect with the afterlife like she claimed she occasionally did, or if she was simply a con artist, but there was no denying her high success rate where predictions were concerned. Emily often said that Amelia was just a good guesser. Jason didn't know if he agreed with that or not.

It could be, he thought, not for the first time. *Maybe she's just winging it. But she does turn out right an awful amount of the time.*

Sometimes Amelia seemed completely genuine to him, and at other times she seemed nothing more than a snake-oil saleswoman, with her long black hair and exotic makeup, her long strangely painted robes and arcane jewelry and talk of disembodied spirits and the ether.

But none of that right now, Jason thought, with a smile Amelia which clearly misinterpreted as his either approval of something she'd said or done, or of her beautiful self in general. *She's dressed exactly like the rest of us, in boots and khaki and denim. Obviously, when you step into the woods, you can't really do so wearing a long robe; and if you wore a looped necklace of exotic beads, said beads are very likely to snag on a low-hanging branch at some point and wind up too scattered across the forest floor to collect again.*

"Well, looks like we got one tent set up," Amelia said brightly; once again giving Jason the come-hither look she'd been favoring him with all day.

Suddenly feeling better about things, Jason disconnected the pump and then he and Amelia got to work setting up the second and larger tent the men would be sleeping in.

As they worked, Jason Reynolds felt intensely relieved that he was thinking of other things than hurting or killing everyone.

God damn Agent Orange. I wish for the life of me that I could ditch the damn thing!

And Amelia worked along beside him, seemingly completely unaware of her companion's mental turmoil.

"Hey, this is just like the TV series 'Finding Bigfoot,' " Jason said after a while.

"Yeah," Amelia agreed. "Except that they never did find him, and we most likely will tomorrow."

"Please show some respect," Professor Marshall called out. 'That was a great show.''

Jason and Amelia gave each other a knowing smile. They knew Professor Marshall was close friends with BFRO president Matt Moneymaker, who'd headed the investigative team on the Animal Planet cryptid series.

"Well anyway, it looks like we'll soon have our own TV show too," Emily said, looking up from her computer programming with a satisfied expression on her face. "Personally, I can't wait."

After Jason and Amelia had been working for a while at setting up both tents' guy ropes, Amelia straightened up, wiped some sweat from her brow, and told Jason: "You know, and I'm serious this time, I really do hope Bonnie B. is still alive."

"Me too," Jason agreed.

Ameila touched her chest at the base of her neck and sighed: "I keep getting the feeling that she is alive at this moment, somewhere close by in these mountains." Then she looked around at the slowly dimming clearing. "But I also wonder what kind of condition she'll be in after all this while. It's been close to a month now that she's been gone, and if she's been with bigfoot all that while . . ."

Jason nodded. "Yeah, I know. We'll let's hope for Bonnie B. Wilde's sake that bigfoot isn't as well hung or as horny as monster porn tends to make out."

Amelia laughed at that. "Yeah, that's right. Otherwise, I can't begin to imagine what her pus—"

"Guys, give it a rest, will you?" Emily interrupted them with her usual serious expression. "Please stop making Mr. Biggie out to be a slut."

Jason and Amelia stared at the doctor in surprise for a moment and then burst into joint peals of laughter.

CHAPTER 6

Amelia's suspicions were quite correct. At that very moment the intrepid cryptid researcher and YouTuber Bonnie B. Wilde was still very much alive. She was also close by, less than a hundred yards away in fact, though neither she nor the team of bigfoot researchers had any idea of this.

Despite being alive and mostly unharmed, however, Bonnie wasn't in good spirits.

First off, Bonnie B. Wilde was currently a prisoner in her sasquatch captor's underground lair. And for the foreseeable future she saw no chance of her escaping her prison. This particular bigfoot (she had no idea if the same held true for all of the species) lived in a hole in the ground, one that was closed off to the world by a massive rock. Once in place, the rock lay quite deep in the earth and was of such a size as to discourage thoughts that it concealed a cave.

As far as Bonnie was concerned, she had no chance in hell of shifting that rock and making her escape.

But the sasquatch had no difficulty in using the massive rock as a door, constantly rolling it aside whenever he went outside. But he also rolled the stone back in place once he was outside the door, after each time first giving Bonnie a stare that warned, "Now you stay exactly where you are until I get back home."

Home? She thought now, casting her anguished gaze around the cave. *Yeah, I guess a stupid creature like bigfoot would consider this place an appropriate residence.*

The cave was quite spacious, large enough that when bigfoot stood in its most cramped section, which was over in the corner he used as a toilet, there was still about a foot between the creature's head and the ceiling. In the rest of the cave, that space would be about four feet. The rock which sealed them both in lay in the corner opposite the toilet space, and was accessed by a set of roughly hewn steps, which spoke of bigfoot's rudimentary intelligence.

The rock didn't completely cover the cave entrance, letting in, along with air, a degree of daylight and moonlight, which in addition to letting Bonnie see around her, had enabled her to mark the passing of time.

Twenty-nine days now. Twenty-nine fucking days I've been locked up in this place by this oafish beast!

Bonnie stared ruefully at her giant captor, who lay on his side, with his face to the wall. Oh, how many times during her month-long incarceration had she fantasized about bashing his head in with a rock, while he slept. But she'd never given in to the urge, for two reasons. The first was that, even though the cave did have an abundance of rocks she could have used as a weapon, she doubted she could kill bigfoot anyway. At the most, Bonnie suspected she'd just make bigfoot mad and then he'd punish her in some beastly way.

The second reason why Bonnie had so far made no attempt to kill bigfoot while he slept was because doing so would really accomplish nothing. Even if she killed bigfoot, she still had no way of shifting the rock that sealed them down here.

So, like now, she sat waiting, hoping and praying that she got away before she shared the fate of the dead woman whose withered body lay over in the far corner.

No, bigfoot hadn't killed the woman; her dead body revealed no evidence of violence to Bonnie's eyes. Bonnie suspected that the woman had just fallen sick and bigfoot had been unable to understand that she needed to be let out of his home until she died.

But that's bad enough, she thought as bigfoot let out a loud series of snores. *The same thing could very well happen to me!*

The cave stank. Other than always going to the toilet in the same part of the cave, bigfoot clearly had no concept of human hygiene. Dung was piled high in the toilet region, and Bonnie often found herself stamping on bugs and worms that had strayed away from there. The other smell was bigfoot's own smell, a thick reek of sweat and urine and pungent animal musk that Bonnie was only now getting used to.

Bonnie was naked. Even if she had had clothes, she would have removed them herself, because this cave was generally warm, sometimes unbearably so. All she'd been wearing for the past month were her panties. The panties were Bonnie's sole concession to modesty. Bigfoot had no idea what they were, and since to Bonnie's relief, the creature had made no attempts to ravish her since abducting her, Bonnie kept the panties on.

So, for the moment, Bonnie was alive and quite well. She wasn't about going hungry. Bigfoot plied her with lots of food, mostly fruit, nuts, and some dead animals, including raccoons, which she of course refused to eat. Drinking water came from the small brook that flowed through the cave in the corner opposite the toilet area, the cave entrance and exit of which were regrettably both too narrow to allow an escape attempt.

So, all Bonnie did now was eat, sleep, hope she wasn't getting fat and ugly from being stuck down here with fat and ugly bigfoot, and hope someone would come looking for her.

She'd somehow managed to hold onto her cellphone while being abducted, but she'd never been able to call civilization from underground here, and in a week the phone battery had run out anyway.

Accelerating the drain on Bonnie's cellphone battery had been her desire to make a video record of bigfoot's residence and personal habits. While filming both, she'd realized that once she escaped from here the video footage would be priceless; but the enthusiasm resulting from that knowledge had unfortunately led to her exhausting her phone's battery power.

Bigfoot grunted in his sleep and rolled over. Bonnie looked at him and sighed. After the first incident of his publicly spraying her with semen he'd left her alone. She'd since figured out that the public masturbation and semen spraying was part of the sasquatch ritual of claiming a female, one that was performed after defeating a rival male, which would in this case be her boyfriend Donnie.

But since then bigfoot had had made no attempts to sexually molest her. The creature didn't seem to be much more intelligent that a well-trained dog, but to Bonnie's relief, it at least understood that if it copulated with her, the massive size of its penis might kill her. Or maybe it simply couldn't detect the opening to copulate with, mistaking her vagina for her urethra. She suspected female sasquatches would have a vagina large enough to stick one's arm in up to the elbow.

What the hell had happened to Donnie anyway? Bonnie wasn't holding out much hope for his survival. She seen him racing after herself and bigfoot and then sudden vanish from sight like he'd fallen off the figurative edge of the world. She doubted Donnie had survived; because if he had, he'd surely have led a rescue team out here searching for her. He loved her and wouldn't ever give up searching for her.

But for a whole month she'd sat near the cave entrance hoping to hear the sound of external voices, but to no avail.

So for the moment, all Bonnie B. Wilde could do was stare angrily at bigfoot's hairy almost-human face, and occasionally, to distract herself, wonder how much her YouTube followers were missing her.

After a while, the anger and misery of Bonnie's predicament became too much for her to bear and she began weeping.

CHAPTER 7

Professor Marshall had long been aware that something was wrong with Jason Reynolds. He couldn't claim to be psychic like Amelia was, but he'd known Jason for too many years not to notice the radical shifts in the reporter's behavior, despite Jason's efforts to conceal what was going on.

For instance, the Jason he'd known and worked with, these past few years was a very meticulous person, a man dedicated to getting things right. On past bigfoot hunting expeditions it had always been one of Marshall's comforts that he knew someone was watching all the details.

Yes, Emily and James handled the technological side of things. Emily took care of the digital stuff and James the mechanical aspect of their expeditions, while Amelia helped him out with valuable advice and her feelings, and also helped with catering; but Jason had always been the one who had the checklist. Jason it was who ensured they had everything they needed, who crosschecked the inventory, and who made certain they never shied away from either performing those tasks that were considered unpleasant, or from making a detailed search for their target even when they were discouraged by their lack of success.

But now . . .

Inside the tent the men would be sharing, Marshall paused searching his backpack for a power bank to recharge his phone with, and reflected on the day's happenings. *Overnight the guy has grown sloppy, like God reached down from heaven and jerked the backbone out of him. I'm not sure what's wrong with him, but I've got my suspicions.*

Professor Marshall was particularly smarting because Jason hadn't brought along the infrared spectrometer, which Emily had specifically stated they would need on this quest. The "IS Unit" was a device that mapped all living creatures above ground within a 50-yard radius, regardless of foliage or terrain. Marshall had gotten the unit, which hadn't been used for a while, out of storage and handed it to Jason for safekeeping during their trip. The theory for use on this trip was to set up camp in the area where the camera was found and run the IS Unit at varying periods to see what all might be lurking nearby, yet just out of plain site.

I gave it to him right before we left my house. How in the hell could he have left it behind?

Jason claimed to have left the IS Unit in Marshall's bathroom, where he had set it down when he went to pee.

Marshall was already having his doubts that Jason had actually gone to do his business in his bathroom.

Just like earlier this evening when he claimed his shoelace had come undone, and then lagged behind the rest of us for the next ten minutes! How long does it take to tie a shoelace? And then there's the fact that he seems very shaky, like he's holding himself together only by willpower.

Those were worrying signs of his friend and cameraman's possible drug use and addiction, but as Professor Benjamin Marshall connected his cellphone to the power bank, there was something else that found even more worrying:

No, don't tell me I'm the only one who's noticing this—but why do the guy's eyes have that orange tint? It wasn't so noticeable before, but now it's almost like Jason washes his eyes with orange soda each morning.

Professor Marshall quickly reached the conclusion that he needed to talk to Jason about this, before the man's erratic behavior jeopardized their entire expedition.

And there's the fact that when he rejoined us this afternoon after supposedly 'tying his shoelaces,' I sense a marked character shift in him. He seemed angry, almost enraged; at a point I felt scared that he'd attack me. I really need to talk this over with Jason before . . . but, dammit, how on earth could he have forgotten to bring the IS Unit?

CHAPTER 8

After a while of striding purposefully along the riverside, and looking at the nearby cabins for any irregularities, ranger Gary Bentley paused and sat on a conveniently placed park bench. From this vantage point he stared across the river, attempting to penetrate the thick cover of woods and see those campsites that had been set up near to the river.

He got no voyeuristic thrill from this action; it was merely to ensure everyone was safe, and there were no clearly apparent fire hazards. Watching from this point gave Gary a wide-ranging panorama that enabled him to take in the whole sweep of the campground almost at a single glance.

Then, after satisfying himself that all was well across the river, Gary turned his attention upward on his side of the river. Staring up the mountainside, he tried to work out where Professor Marshall and his team would be setting up camp.

Now Gary was amused. Ben Marshall was one of those kooky individuals who had an almost religious reverence for bigfoot. Gary had met him several times over the years in the woods, always researching some odd creature the Native Americans or early settlers had once believed to exist.

To Gary's mind, bigfoot seemed the least odd of the things Ben Marshall believed in.

And now he's led his team up the side of the mountain, saying he's sure bigfoot lives up there somewhere!

Gary laughed heartily. *Folks can be so funny sometimes. Imagine Marshall, a college professor in his fifties, looking for a fabled creature. And with such great dedication too.*

But that was exactly what had happened. Marshall, his tracker cousin James, two female researchers and another guy Gary thought he'd recently seen on TV, had all lugged their weird gear up there this afternoon. Gary had escorted them part of the way and told them he'd check on them from time to time to ensure they were okay.

Gary was conscientious in that way. Even here at the Sleepaway Campground phone signals often proved sketchy, and up there where the good professor was currently camping, your cellphone simply wouldn't work at all.

Most days, Gary couldn't even get the ranger station on his walkie-talkie when he was that far up the mountainside. So Gary felt he needed to check on the professor and his associates, just in case they got into some unforeseen difficulty and needed an emergency intervention and retrieval.

But still, he thought in amusement as he resumed his short trek downriver to the next bridge, *nothing bad's gonna happen to Ben Marshall and his team of college nerds. What could possibly happen to them? It's not like they're gonna run into bigfoot when he's cracked out on Agent Orange.*

That thought cracked Gary Bentley up and he laughed heartily all the way back across the river and over to the car park and his ranger truck.

CHAPTER 9

Campfire time. Almost everyone was exhausted after the day's long hike, but no one liked to miss the familiar feeling of sitting around the campfire and sharing stories.

So they sat around the campfire on a mixture of camping chairs and tree stumps, eating Amelia's sandwiches and drinking warm beer, the icebox in Professor Marshall's recreational vehicle having been considered an unnecessary burden to lug up the mountainside.

"All in all, it's been a good day, if you ask me," James Gallagher said after a while of staring into the orange flames. We've reached our destination and set up both our camp and our instruments."

Emily nodded. "I agree with you. Sniffy reveals a higher level of musky or odiferous animal secretions than what I consider normal for this altitude, which I'm interpreting to mean this forest environment contains a specific disrupting factor. And that disrupting factor can only be our elusive friend bigfoot." Before continuing with what she was saying, she looked between Marshall and James, both seated opposite her, and her gaze descended the darkened mountain slope to where several distant orange glows marked out the campfires burning at the Sleepaway Campground. "So, I'm certain we're in the right place, and with any luck we'll shortly have the first properly documented human encounter with a sasquatch."

"And then it'll be glory days and champagne and caviar for all of us," James mumbled around his mouthful of bread, cheese, and lettuce. "We five will all be lauded like kings and serenaded like queens." He swallowed, burped into his hand, and then laughed. "And I for one can't wait to be celebrated. It'll be great payback for all the fruitless expeditions we've embarked on over the years, trying to catch bigfoot on camera. I ain't gonna lie, more than once, I've been this fucking close to quitting this group. I was almost losing my faith in the existence of cryptids altogether."

Before biting into his sandwich again, he sighed. "I'm just hopin' this isn't another wild goose chase that we're on, that inconceivable as it seems from the evidence we've got, Bonnie B. and Donnie, didn't just fake the whole thing." James suddenly raised his voice and yelled into the forest. "Hey, biggie! You'd better be nearby, or I'm gonna be really pissed off."

"Oh, he's definitely nearby," Amelia said, finally sitting down with the others with a plate of food in her lap. "I sense the vibes strongly now." Then she looked pensive. "Of course, since we're talking here about a living creature and not a disembodied being, I'm limited in what I sense. But I have a clear feeling that our little group here is gonna have the closest of encounters with our sasquatch friend. Maybe the closest human-sasquatch encounter ever."

"I'm damn glad to hear that, sister!" James said, toasting her with his beer can.

Professor Marshall had been listening to the others. Now, with his plate empty, he said: "I really wish I knew what perfume Bonnie B. was wearing that day."

"Huh?" Amelia laughed and then asked: "What's her perfume got to do with it?"

"Uh . . . well . . . uh . . ." Professor Marshall suddenly looked distracted and stopped speaking, and so, after a short pause, it was Emily who answered Amelia's question. "Oh, you know, lots of modern perfumes have pheromones mixed into them. What Ben is suggesting is that possibly, bigfoot was attracted to Bonnie B. Wilde because of a specific pheromone or combination of pheromones that made it horny. Remember what it did before carrying Bonnie off?"

Amelia's nose wrinkled up in disgust. "The cum-shower bath? Ugh, like I could ever forget." She looked towards Marshall for confirmation. "Is that what you were gonna—hey, professor, what's the matter."

Professor Marshall was staring to Amelia's right and soon everyone else was too. All eyes fell on Jason, who'd been silent since their group had taken their places around the campfire. There was clearly something wrong with Jason, who was shivering like he had a fever. His face looked all wrong too, like he was in a trance, and now that all attention was focused on him, everyone saw that their cameraman hadn't eaten a single bite of the two large sandwiches Amelia had served him.

"Hey, Jason, what's the matter with you?" Amelia asked in alarm, putting down her own plate and nudging him with her hand.

Jason surfaced like a man coming out of a trance. "I'm . . . I'm . . . okay," he sputtered, like he had a mouthful of beer, when in actuality his beer hung unopened in his slack hand and looked like it would fall to the ground at any moment. "I'm just . . ."

Professor Marshall got up and walked around the fire to Jason's side. He crouched by the man and stared into his eyes, which, with their tint amplified by the reflected of the campfire, now had more than a hint of the orange color he'd previously noticed.

Shaking his head, he got to his feet again. "This is worse than I imagined," he mumbled to himself.

Jason sat there, looking unsteady, swaying like a leaf in a high wind.

Hey, dude," James Gallagher said before the professor could speak, "what exactly the hell is wrong with you? You look like you got a monkey on your back."

"Yes," Emily instantly agreed, "and not the kind of ape that swings in the trees either."

In response, Jason began to get to his feet. "I need to go lie down," he said.

But Professor Marshall restrained Jason in his chair with a firm hand on his shoulder. "Not yet, my dear friend," the professor said. "I think we need to talk this out."

Jason let himself be forced down onto his seat, but shook his head weakly. "There's nothing to talk about. I'll be fine once I—"

"Once you shoot up?" James asked with a cold smirk. "Dude, you're shaking like a junkie doing cold turkey. What is the matter with you?"

Jason shook his head again, and once more began denying that anything was the matter, but then he noticed the professor's eyes on him. Those elderly bespectacled eyes held great wisdom, but also great concern for him.

"Oh, my friend, I think you'd better tell us all what's going on," the professor said. "You're in danger of seriously compromising and jeopardizing our mission here. In fact, you've already begun messing up our expedition."

"I have?" Jason asked in surprise. "But I haven't done anything to anyone?"

"You forgot to bring along the IS Unit. Now I'll have to drive back to town for it."

Now Emily looked coldly at Jason. "You forgot the ISU? How could you? You know how essential that is to this chase."

"Calm down, Em," Amelia said, walking over to stand with a hand on Jason's shoulder. "We can thank God the professor remembered it in time. It would have been disastrous to encounter bigfoot without the ISU on us, as he might very well keep on eluding us."

"What I want to know is how you, Jason—who are normally the most detail-minded of us all—could forget something so damned important?" Emily finished anyway.

James nodded. "That's what we all wanna know. Right, Ben?"

Professor Marshall nodded back at him, and then looked down at Jason again. Jason looked up helplessly at the professor, and then around at the others. Then he sighed and asked. "Guys, do I really have to tell you about this?"

"You sure do, man," James smirked back.

Professor Marshall nodded. "Yes, Jason, you do. I too really want to know what the matter is with you."

The two women both nodded as well. And so Jason told them.

***

Jason sighed. "You know, maybe I really should have mentioned this to you guys earlier, but I didn't know where to start from." He shrugged weakly, and then nodded gratefully up at Amelia, who was massaging his shoulders. "You gotta admit it's embarrassing, talking about stuff like this."

He waited for someone to comment, but no one did, so he went on. "Well, what I've got to say is, at the moment I'm an addict. I've got a massive drug problem; a huge monkey on my back, like James described it."

"What drug?" Emily asked.

"Cocaine," Jason replied truthfully. "Or more accurately, crack cocaine."

There were sharp intakes of breath all around. Even Amelia paused in massaging strength back into Jason's body.

"But how did you get into that hard stuff?" Professor Marshall, who was still standing beside Jason, finally asked. "You've always been a clean-cut guy; at most you'd smoke a joint with a friend after a few beers."

"To reply honestly to that question," Jason said, "I blame my own stupidity. I thought I was indestructible, but it proved my undoing." He managed to laugh, then slowly got to his feet and stepped towards the campfire. The air was chilly now, or maybe it was the beginning of another set of shakes. Either way, being close to the fire had the effect of nullifying something obnoxious that threatened to take control of his soul and body.

"My trouble started early this year. I was working with a team investigating a crack house massacre down in South Charleston. On the whole, the investigation was a success."

"I think I saw that on TV," Emily said, but then she looked puzzled. "But how does that apply to you? How'd that turn you into an addict?"

Staring into the depths of the fire, Jason sighed loudly. "Well, if you watched the program, you'll remember the details of the case. Six people killed, including a pregnant mother who was a mule for the drug ring and her two kindergarten-aged kids; each of them riddled with bullet holes."

He laughed grimly, without even a hint of mirth. "Now, okay, I'm a reporter, meaning I've seen a shitload of violence in my day, but on this particular case I got curious in a big way."

"Curious about what, Jason?" Professor Marshall asked.

"Curious about the sort of mental state a person had to be in to kill that many people so bloodily. You remember they caught the guys who did it. Both were crackheads themselves, and had committed the murders simply because they couldn't afford to pay the dealer for their fix. So, they'd killed everyone in the house and taken what they wanted. That murderous level of desperation may have made sense to me on paper, but whenever I got around to really thinking about it, I found myself stumped, and realized I didn't get it at all. No way did it make sense to me that a man would kill a woman and her two kids simply because they needed to get high." He shrugged. "So, being the strong and intrepid reporter that I was, I decided to become a crack addict myself so I could write about it."

He laughed at the shocked looks on his friends' faces. "Yeah, my descent into crack addiction was one hundred percent intentional. At first it was easy, I felt I was in control and believed I could kick the habit anytime I wanted. And I might've been right. But leaving the drug then seemed so easy, that I realized I didn't really have the sort of desperation in me that would lead me to take a human life for my next fix. I needed to go deeper into the heart of human evil . . . and I did . . ."

He looked around at them all, and said. "For better or worse, guys, that's my tale. Now my problem is how to get rid of my addiction."

"Rehab, maybe?" Amelia suggested behind him.

Jason turned from the fire to frown at her. "I'm already booked into the Chestnut Ridge Clinic in Morgantown. Was due to start on their therapy course this week, but then the professor called us up for this sasquatch hunt and it seemed too good an opportunity to pass up." He sighed. "So, what I wanna say to you all is, I'm sorry I'm not up to par at the moment, and I'll do my best to not make any more errors that might fuck up our investigation."

"Shit, man, that's quite some story," James said, as Jason stood there still as a statue. "Takes guts to do what you're doing. Me? Never in a million years would you ever catch me doing crack." He pointed to Professor Marshall. "Ben and I have another cousin, Ron, who got into crack five years ago. Sonofabitch ended up stabbing his wife in the belly when she wouldn't lend him the cash for his next fix."

James lapsed into silence, still shaking his head at Ron's foolishness, and possibly at Jason's foolishness as well.

No one else said anything for a while, until the professor spoke.

"Well, Jason, I'm sure you've learned your lesson now; that playing with fire gets one's fingers burned."

Jason smiled grimly. "Oh, for sure I have. Once, I get through rehab, I'm never touching drugs again." He grinned at Amelia. "Not even some of your bullshit 'psychic marijuana,' woman."

"We're all your friends here, Jason, and we're not gonna judge you," Emily said in a subdued voice. "I for one hope you get yourself sorted out soon."

"That goes for me too," the professor said. "Just let us know if you need any help or anything."

"Just so long as it ain't lending you money for drugs," James said, with a quick laugh. "I ain't about visiting you in the cemetery by contribution to an overdose."

Even Jason laughed at that.

"So, how do you intend to get through this quest if you've no drugs on you?" Emily asked. Then a sudden understanding hit her and she frowned across the clearing at Jason. "Oh, you do have some on you, don't you?"

He nodded back at her. "Just a little bit, but I've been trying not to use it. Which is why I'm this jumpy."

"I think you should use the stuff, man," James said. "No point starving yourself of it before you enter rehab." He paused for a moment, then added. "Just let me know if you're close to freaking out."

"Screw you, bro," Jason said. "I'm not about freaking out."

"My eyes must be deceiving me then."

Professor Marshall intervened before the men's disagreement could degenerate into a quarrel. "Hey, calm down, both of you. Jason, there one more thing I need to understand, though it might not be related to your drug use."

"Yeah? What's that, professor?"

"Your eyes; why are they turning orange?"

Jason looked suddenly tired. "Dunno, prof, I think I must've got a bad batch or something."

"Okay, enough with the interrogating," Amelia told the others. She retrieved Jason's plate of food from where he'd dropped it before getting up to address them all. "Hey, Jason, you gotta eat something, okay? Come over and sit down and eat your sandwiches."

James nodded. "Dammit, man, you're not even drinking your beer."

But Jason shook his head. "Not yet, please, or I'll just throw it up again. Let me step into the tent for a few seconds and fix myself up. Once that's done, I'll be out here and relatively normal."

Without waiting for a reply, he strode away from them into the men's tent.

"Thanks for bringing that up, Ben," James said, once Jason was out of earshot. "I could tell he had the shakes, but didn't wanna mention it for fear of aggravating him. Junkies tend to get cantankerous easily. And besides, I didn't really believe he had a drug problem. A fever could've caused the same symptoms."

"Well, it's resolved now," the professor told them, while both walking back to the wood stump he'd been sitting on and adjusting his glasses on the bridge of his nose. Once seated, he looked first at Emily, then at James. "People, Jason's forgetting the IS Unit means I've got to drive back into town to get it. I'll have to leave now, so I can get back here early enough in the morning that we don't have to waste the day."

The others pondered that for a while, and then James suggested, "Hey, maybe I should go back instead."

But Professor Marshall shook his head. "I think it's best you remain here with the ladies." In reply to James's inquiring nod towards the men's tent, he shook his head. "No, I'm not worried about Jason hurting either of them in a drug rage, but instead about bigfoot abducting one of them. You're good with firearms. I'll feel better leaving the girls well protected here."

"We ladies can look after ourselves," Emily stated a little drunkenly.

The professor nodded. "I'm confident that you can, Em. And I'm equally sure Bonnie B. Wilde said exactly the same thing to Donald before she went missing."

"I personally will feel much safer with James around to protect us," Amelia said.

"So it's settled then," the professor continued. "I'll just get my cellphone from our tent and head down to the RV and . . ."

"I'll come with you down the hillside," James said. "Just to make sure you don't get lost in the dark, then I'll come back up to keep watch over our beautiful female companions."

Emily sighed. "Yeah, I guess that is for the best."

Jason stepped out of the tent then and walked briskly over to his seat.

"Yep. Say all the bad things you like about drugs," he said on sitting down again. "One thing's for sure tho—they do make you feel like a new man."

Then he picked up his previously neglected plate of food and began eating ravenously.

CHAPTER 10

It was ironic that none of the campers sitting around the campfire was aware that the cryptid creature they sought was watching them.

Yes, a bigfoot or sasquatch was standing mere yards away from the humans. He was hidden behind a tree and had instinctively positioned himself downwind from them so they couldn't smell him. Bigfoot wasn't intelligent in any kind of a human way, but he had animal smarts and the learned experience of long age.

To be honest, bigfoot wasn't really interested in the humans anymore. The novelty of their existence had long since worn off. Now the sasquatch species simply considered humanity a nuisance, a sort of noisy (and hairless) far-cousin that bred in prodigious numbers and communicated with strange noises and signs that the bigfoots' animal-level minds found impossible to decipher.

So he/it (and the entire worldwide species) had made a point of leaving the humans alone. The bigfoots weren't an invisible species, but over the centuries they'd mastered the trick of not being seen except they wanted to be.

The human which this particular bigfoot had recently captured was interesting. Her body odor clearly marked her as female, and something about her pleased this particular bigfoot whose own female mate had died in a forest fire many years ago. Since then this bigfoot had lived a lonely life, one that had only been enlivened when he'd captured a previous human female to keep him company.

Admitted that female had been very noisy, and had also been given to strange emotional fits in which large quantities of water began streaming down her face; but still, it had been nice to not be alone again.

(Her female smell had been acceptable to bigfoot, though she was clearly too young [and thus too small] to mate with. Oddly, it seemed that this hairless species of bigfoot never matured past their childhood stage; or why were their female sex organs so small and undeveloped?)

Unfortunately, the human female had gotten bitten by a copperhead and died, leaving bigfoot alone again. That was, until he'd stumbled on his present female captive.

This particular hairless female he had in his home was less troublesome that the previous one, but he could still sense that she wanted to leave him too, and would run away if given the chance.

Seeing as bigfoot didn't want her to desert him, he insisted on sealing the cave each time he left her alone, something he would never have done with a female of his own species.

***

Now, bigfoot watched the campers eat and then talk. There were two females amongst them, but bigfoot had no intention of capturing either of them. One strange female was enough for him, what with their strange dietary requirements. Just like the previous one, this current one also totally refused to eat raw meat, fish, or insects, and insisted on subsisting entirely on fruit and nuts.

But if bigfoot had no interest in the humans he was staring at (whom he had no idea were in the woods for the sole purpose of finding him), there was something they had in their possession which he was very interested in studying.

No, it wasn't their recording equipment; he didn't have the mental capacity to understand anything but the most rudimentary, stone-age level technology. But one of the human males, the tall one with dark brown hair had a substance in his possession that had an unfamiliar smell that was nevertheless quite enticing, like the smell of a fruit the sasquatch had never seen or tasted before, but nonetheless recognized through either an instinctive or an inherited thread of memory.

But since bigfoot was by nature a pacifist creature, and a reclusive sort at that, he wasn't about rushing into the human's camp to search for the source of the tantalizing smell. (His violent display when he'd snatched his current human female companion from her human mate had largely been play-acting triggered by his desperate need to end his loneliness.)

No, in this case, bigfoot would do what his species normally did in such situations; which was wait until the humans had either gone hunting or had fallen asleep, before searching their camp for what he wanted.

But the humans went on communicating in their weird and indecipherable noises and the silent sasquatch soon tired of listening to sounds he didn't understand and waiting for them to fall asleep.

Bigfoot decided to go forage for food and return back here in a little while.

And so, as unnoticed as when he had arrived in the forest near their tents, the monster sasquatch turned and walked away from the cryptid hunters.

CHAPTER 11

Once Professor Marshall had headed downhill with James, Emily finished her drink and said goodnight.

I don't know about you guys, but I'm bushed," she said and then laughed. "I feel like we were walking for hours."

"That's 'cos of all the gear we lugged up here," Jason said.

Emily yawned, waved goodnight, and stepped through the tent flap.

The campfire was already dying down to embers. After a while of sitting side-by-side with Jason in the darkness, Amelia got to her feet and extended her hand towards him. "Come on," she said, "let's go for a walk through the woods. I wanna check out the river."

Jason got to his feet too and took her hand. "What about Emily?" he asked. "The professor is gonna be mad if we leave and something bad happens to her."

But Amelia laughed, the sound of her voice filtering upward and outward through the canopy of trees. "What could possibly happen to her?"

"Bigfoot might come back."

"He won't, unlesss he's planning on exchanging Bonnie B. Wilde for one of us." After a glance towards she and Emily's tent, she tugged on Jason's hand. "Come on, man. I don't really wanna look at the fucking river. There's something I wanna show you."

He smiled at her. "Why not show me here?"

She rolled her eyes. "Because, Jason, it's not something I want Emily to see."

Jason followed her off into the surrounding woods. After they'd been walking a short distance, Amelia pulled out a joint and lit up.

"You've gotta be kidding me," Jason said, while shifting tree branches out of their way. "Is this what you wanted to show me?"

She passed the joint to him. "Dude, shut up and take a hit."

Jason took a hit of the marijuana. The drug did little for him, but he didn't mind. He still had the pack of Agent Orange in his back pocket, and could renew his high anytime he wanted by simply breaking out a chunk of orange 'candy' to chew on. But he didn't want to do so now.

Maybe talking to the others purged me, 'cos I do feel quite relaxed, he told himself as Amelia led him further away from their pair of tents.

She led them so far off in fact, that Jason began thinking they'd never find their way back to their campsite; that was, until he remembered Amelia's psychic ability. Where recalling landmarks and finding directions was concerned, Amelia was almost as good as James was; with the added advantage in her case that she didn't need to have a specific starting point to return to.

Amelia could navigate her way by pure instinct. *Like during that expedition to the Montana backwoods last year when we all got lost.*

Yes, I feel more relaxed tonight than at any other time since I made the horrible acquaintance of Agent Orange. Maybe rehab will help me; but dammit, I doubt it. I didn't dare tell Ben it's Agent Orange I'm addicted to, not regular street crack. Oh, damn, what the hell am I gonna do?

But by now, he'd taken a few more hits of the joint, before passing it back to Amelia, and the THC had begun to kick it. Now he began to feel mellow, like he really didn't need the Agent Orange anymore. Back in a small corner of his mind he knew he was deceiving himself by thinking this way, but it was a better state of mind to be in than constantly imagining how one day he'd be out of his mind, locked up in the penitentiary for killing someone, or worst of all . . . dead of an overdose with his brains popped into orange popcorn.

Amelia led them both to a cliff edge over which they could see the Tygart Valley River shimmering below. Almost like she'd planned this beforehand, here the grass was low like it was freshly mown and the tree line began well back from the sheer drop into space.

"And now for what I wanted to show you," she said coyly, turning away from him and wagging her ass at him like a stripper just beginning her show.

Jason watched her peel away her clothes with her back to him. She was swaying like the marijuana was ramping up her slight intoxication from the beers she'd already drunk, but they were both ten yards in from the edge of the mountain; far enough that he didn't have to worry about her falling over the cliff edge.

He knew what she wanted from him and intended to give it to her.

Thank heavens, Agent Orange doesn't kill a guy's sex drive. That's something to be thankful for.

He realized then he'd known Amelia Blackwood for ten years by this point, and yet never once had they gotten as close as this. He also realized that their not hooking up earlier had been accidental rather than intentional. There had been enough attraction between them to cause them to date one another. But, somehow over the intervening years, each time one of them was single, the other one had a partner; and neither of them had ever felt like cheating on their partner.

It's like the fates kept us apart from each other until tonight. Well, whatever their reasons, I'm all for it now.

Amelia finally got her clothes completely off. When they all lay by her feet, she spun around in their midst and flung out her hands to her sides. Her body was compact and tight, exactly like Jason had sometimes imagined it would be. Firm thighs, small breasts and toned limbs.

"How'd you like my surprise?" she asked him with a broad smile on her face.

"I fucking love it."

"Then get undressed, baby, and hurry it up."

Jason got undressed and did hurry it up. Then he hurried over to Amelia and they both got down to having hot and sweaty sex.

Both were unaware that less than a mile away, bigfoot was nearing them.

CHAPTER 12

After making love to Amelia, Jason fell asleep. After his orgasm a sense of complete wellbeing flooded through him and he lay back on the grass.

Amelia kissed Jason on the lips and then, feeling the call of nature, headed into the forest to relieve herself.

On returning from peeing, Amelia walked slowly over to where their clothes were piled. She felt soothed, the fucking had released a lot of sexual tension. It had been two months since she'd been with a man, and before getting together with Jason tonight, she'd wondered how long she could endure the dry spell she'd been on.

Before bending to pick up her clothes, she gave Jason a tender look. Though rushed, the sex had been very nice; and she looked forward to doing it again with him before they headed back to the campsite.

That is, if I can even wake him up. The guy looks unconscious, not just asleep. Fuck . . . where'd I put that other damn joint?

She'd not brought a handbag on this short hike, and had stashed both joints in her jeans' pockets; one for before sex, the other for after. But now, she could feel something else in her pants' pocket, something she didn't remember putting in there.

She pulled whatever it was out and took a good look at it. A medium-sized package of what seemed—in the available moonlight—pink or orange candy. Puzzled as to how the candies had gotten into her jeans, Amelia put one in her mouth, and bit into it.

Ugh! She immediately spat it out. It had an unpleasant 'chemical' taste to it, like something made for cleaning hospital floors.

Then, staring at the package, she realized what had happened.

I just mixed up my jeans for Jason's. Yeah, fuck me, I'm stoned, aren't I? But so, what was that crap I just tasted?

Amelia thought for a bit and then finally understood that she'd stumbled on Jason's stash of crack cocaine.

But I thought crack was white in color. But this stuff . . .

But now Amelia realized she'd gotten distracted from her true objective here at their pile of clothes, which was to find the second joint, fire up, and then go to sleep beside her new lover, who was now contentedly dozing a few yards away from her.

Then we'll have great sex in the morning, and sneak back into the camp before sunrise. Nothing bad can possibly happen to Emily before James gets back from walking the professor down to his car, and so long as sweet Emily is alive and well for Professor Marshall to fawn over, James won't ever tell that we left her alone. Besides, now that I'm half-stoned, there's no way I'll ever correctly backtrack the route we reached here by. We'll just get completely lost, turned around over and over again.

That seemed good enough to Amelia. Once she found the joint, she got it lit and then sat on the grass smoking her marijuana and getting high as a bird and tripping out on the expanded psychic vibes the THC in the joint seemed to give her. Amelia already sensed the world with more perception than regular people; and yet marijuana seemed to expand on her perceptivity even further.

Sitting naked cross-legged on the grass, Amelia smoked the joint down to the roach. Then she realized that she was still holding onto Jason's package of crack cocaine.

She considered returning the package into his jeans for safe-keeping, but then the imp of the perverse stirred in her breast and she got up.

"He doesn't need drugs anymore now that he's got me," she said. A comment which of course seemed perfectly logical to her THC-reconfigured state of mind.

And that comment made, Amelia Blackwood took careful aim and tossed Jason's precious package of Agent Orange as far as she could into the woods. Which surprisingly, was very far indeed.

Far enough in fact, that bigfoot came upon the package without even looking for it.

Once Amelia had dispatched the crack cocaine into the trees, she dropped the roach onto the grass and unsteadily walked over to Jason's side and lay down beside him to get some sleep.

She was of course completely unaware of the momentous disaster that she'd just inadvertently set in motion.

CHAPTER 13

Bigfoot was on his way back over to the human camp, when the very smell he was on his way to investigate made him change direction.

For a brief period, he stood motionless, his little brain confused. A faint trace of the unfamiliar odor still reached him from far off; and that same smell also seemed to be coming from nearby.

Bigfoot decided to investigate the nearer occurrence of the odor first, and so he turned aside into the trees.

It was a very short trip to the object he sought, and very soon he was picking up a small metal tin from the forest floor.

Up close the little package smelled even better and instinctively the sasquatch found himself emptying the contents of the package into his mouth and chewing on them.

True, this soft orange food didn't taste as nice as it smelt, but its fantastic odor more than compensated for this deficiency.

Soon the package was empty, and bigfoot found himself suddenly filled with an unfamiliar and very strange anxiety.

He had a bad headache and his belly hurt him just as badly.

Worst of all, he was now having difficulty thinking straight.

And so, with the dangerous orange drug he had just eaten making its strange and disastrous changes in his brain and his body, bigfoot headed off in the one direction he clearly remembered.

He made his way back towards his cave, where his human female mate waited.

Maybe his captive would be able to help him.

And along the way, as he stumbled home, his mind became more and more strange and deranged.

By the time bigfoot arrived back at his cave, the drug known as Agent Orange had almost completed its evil work of transforming this normally gentle and retiring old creature into an extremely dangerous monster.

It had also turned his eyes to a glowing and brilliant orange color, the most obvious sign of a maniacal Agent Orange addict.

CHAPTER 14

Bonnie B. Wilde was almost falling asleep on her bed of grass and leaves when she heard the sound of the great stone that blocked off the cave entrance being rolled away.

By now this was a very familiar sound to her, and one that she would normally ignore, except if they were low on food in the cave and she was hungry, as she knew that her sasquatch captor placed a top priority on keeping her well-fed.

She had long ago given up her daydreams of sneaking out of her prison and escaping back to rejoin human society, on a day when bigfoot forgot to seal off his cave. This was one area of his life in which the huge hairy creature was unerringly meticulous.

But tonight, something felt different about bigfoot's return to their cave. For a moment Bonnie disinterestedly tried to work out what the difference was.

But once she realized what she was hearing, she quickly sat up.

She listened again just to make sure. Yes, it was true. Where usually, bigfoot had no difficulty whatsoever in rolling away the door to his cave, tonight it was taking him longer than normal. Bonnie could hear the creature huffing and puffing away and grunting fiercely as he worked the cave entrance open.

And then, when he finally did roll the rock back and had entered the cave, bigfoot made no attempt to lever the massive object back into place as he normally did.

Instead, while clutching his head as if it hurt him badly, Bigfoot stumbled down the stone stairs and wobbled his way towards his bed, where he then collapsed on his side, and then lay staring at Bonnie from eyes that seemed larger than normal and also grossly deformed in some way. Also, he now began gasping as if in severe pain, and let out a long stream of urine from his much-larger-than-normal member, which, in contrast to its usual flaccid state and the miserable state of its owner, seemed to be growing erect.

For a split second, Bonny B. Wilde stood conflicted. She could see clearly that the door to her freedom had finally opened in her favor. And yet, she was basically a kind person. Even though the sasquatch had held her captive for a month, his suffering state tugged at her heartstrings and she wished she could do something to relieve his suffering.

Indeed, Bonnie had unconsciously already begun walking over to bigfoot's side to attempt to comfort him. But then she remembered the withered female corpse that lay near bigfoot's toilet.

Oh heck no, she thought as a desperate spear of dread stabbed through her at her memory of the dead woman's taut and rotted face. *I'm getting the fuck out of here while the getting is good!*

Bigfoot was still rolling on the floor and whimpering in pain.

"Sorry, dude, but I need to get back to human civilization," Bonnie said as she dashed past bigfoot, on a one-way trip to the steps. "There's no way for me to call a doctor for you, but I really hope you feel better in the morning."

As she passed bigfoot, he reached out to grab her ankle, but Bonnie successfully evaded his clutching hairy hand and ran up the stairs and out into the night.

Then, overcome with emotion, she stopped running and burst into tears instead.

"I'm free! Oh yes, I'm free. Free at last!"

Bonnie peeked back into the cave. Bigfoot still lay on the floor, whimpering loudly and making no attempt to come after her. Bonnie was relieved by this, as it meant that for the time being, her captor could be ruled out of making any attempt to recapture her.

With that settled, her next impulse was to phone for help.

Dammit, she thought in anger, on realizing that in her desperate hurry to exit the cave, she had forgotten to grab her cell phone.

Fuck no, I'm not reentering that cave for all the money in the world. But fuck, if I had my phone I could call Donnie to come get me. But then she corrected herself: No you couldn't, you idiot. For one thing, the damn phone is out of battery power, because you kept trying to call for help, and kept filming bigfoot's cave. And second, there's no damn phone signal on this damn mountain anyway.

Then Bonnie laughed. "But who needs cell phones anyway? I'm free, free, free! All I need to do is make it down to the Sleepaway Campground and borrow a phone from someone there."

After one last glance through the cave entrance at her erstwhile captor, Bonnie B. Wilde hurried down the mountainside.

CHAPTER 15

A tent in the woods . . . a short while later.

Dr. Emily Thompson was in the center of an erotic dream. Such dreams were no strangers to Emily's nighttime subconscious, because, being a woman who hardly ever dated, she always had an excessive amount of sexual tension to work out.

And seeing as Emily Thompson was obsessed with cryptids, her nighttime erotic fantasies always tended to skew in this direction. In the past she'd had erotic trysts with aliens and demons and one time even the Mothman.

But her favorite dream lover was bigfoot. There was just something about bigfoot that made Emily imagine him as the ultimate love machine, the one individual fully equipped to satisfy her more than any woman had ever been sexually satisfied before.

Just like tonight.

In tonight's fantasy, Emily was an intrepid cryptid explorer being pursued by a lusty tribe of inbred rednecks, who were seeking to recapture her after her daring escape from their hillside compound, where they'd enslaved her and forced her to cook disgusting meals for her. She'd been hiding from them behind a tree, but worse luck, had startled a bird, which had then alerted the inbred rednecks to her nearby presence.

Now, the rednecks, their deformed lips slavering with spittle, their deformed eyes gaping with glee, had her encircled and were closing in.

One of them touched her with his filthy six-finger hand and voila!—because this was a dream, all of Emily's clothes immediately vanished.

"Help!" Emily screamed. Then she smote the deformed man in the face. "Don't you dare touch me!"

But her words had no effect on her attacker. The redneck stepped in close and began slobbering greedily on Emily's left breast, sucking the nipple into his hair lip and trying to bite it off.

A second, equally deformed redneck—this one completely bald and sporting a beard that reached to his knees, grabbed hold of Emily's second breast and sucked its entirety into his mouth. A third redneck—this one a dwarf that barely reached Emily's waist, took advantage of his physical shortcomings to place his lips over Emily's clitoris and begin sucking.

"Let me go!" Emily shrieked as she felt her body begin to betray her, and felt the pleasure her captors intended her to feel. She was burning with desire, but also with shame now. These rednecks had enslaved her mind and were now seeking to transfer this sexual domination to her body. She must resist, she must resist them . . .

But already Emily knew she was undone. Yet another redneck was stripping off his denim overalls, leaving himself dressed in just his dirty old boots. But the man had a massive cock, which hung down to his knees.

"I'm gonna tear your ass to shreds with ma member, bitch!" the man laughed at her, rubbing his cock so it quickly began hardening. "Yeah, I certainly am gonna do just that to your asshole."

Emily knew that if this man stuck his giant penis into her ass, she'd be finished, forever the sex slave of these deformed people. Already, she was slipping deeper into the well of pleasure created by their trio of mouths sucking on her nipples and clitoris.

"Somebody, please help me! I need a hero now! I'll pay you with pussy!" she screamed in erotic desperation.

And then, as the incredibly hung man stepped towards her, he began growing in stature. Suddenly he was eight feet tall and covered in hair. He still had the same giant penis, but it no longer reached down to his knees like it had when he'd been a human being. Now his cock was in perfectly proportion to the rest of his body.

Emily wept with tears of joy, as she realized what had happened. Oh, it was bigfoot. He'd heard her pleas and disguised himself as one of the horny rednecks so he could save her.

And save her he did. There was no fight at all. Once bigfoot growled at Emily's ravishers, they all took to their heels. The dwarf didn't run fast enough, so bigfoot kicked him in the britches, sending him flying through the air like a punted football.

Then bigfoot lay Emily down on a soft bed of grass and moss and inserted himself deep into her now-dripping womanhood.

"Oh, yes, darling, I need you in me so bad. I'm gonna love you the rest of my life," Emily gushed in pleasure as bigfoot now fucked the shit out of her.

Normally, this was as far as Dr. Emily Thompson's bigfoot sexual fantasy went. But tonight was different, because, at the point in the dream where she normally had her dream orgasm and woke up, she felt something poking her between her legs. The thing had a blunt head, and quickly nudged its way between her dream-wetted labia and into her vagina.

It took Emily a few seconds to realize that she was being fucked for real.

But when she opened her eyes to see exactly who was violating her, she saw that it was *BIGFOOT*. He was kneeling over her, hairy as ever, and the tip of his cock, which was even longer and fatter than that of the dream bigfoot, was already inside her.

And it hurt!

But then Emily Thompson felt relieved that she was still dreaming. She knew this to be the case, because, despite the slowly growing pain in her birth canal, and the musky animal stink that now filled the tent, this particular bigfoot had glowing orange eyes—eyes as large as tennis balls in fact—and being an expert on cryptids, Emily knew that real-life bigfoots never had orange eyes that glowed in the dark like lamps.

So yes, she was still dreaming. But if this was a dream, then why the hell was she hurting so much?

"Oh, take it easy, honey, you're hurting me," Emily pleaded. "Your cock is so big—if you carry on like this, you're going to split me completely in half."

Bigfoot grunted and appeared to grin at her, then he withdrew his erection a few inches, which made Emily sigh in relief.

"Yes, honey, that's so much better," she moaned, with sweat dripping down her brow.

If I'm still dreaming, why is it so damned hot in here? The sweat is streaming off of me like I'm in a sauna!

The sensation she now felt was a dizzying one, one that hovered on the borderline between pleasure and pain. His body balanced on his massive hairy arms, Bigfoot hovered over her, his three-foot-long penis the bridge connecting them.

"Oh yes, yes, baby," Emily moaned. "I think I'm gonna co—"

Then bigfoot made a long thrust into her body and her eyes widened as his member burst through the end of her vagina and ripped her womb to shreds.

Emily felt something inside of her pop like a bubble, and she screamed. Her continuing fantasy dissolved. Now there was no pretense of this being a dream. She understood that she was wide awake—indeed had been wide awake ever since the first penile insertion—and that bigfoot—her long lusted after Mr. Biggie, was actively raping her.

And as he pulled out his member again and thrust it back in, further ripping up her insides, Emily realized that there was more to this bigfoot rape than mere lust.

His eyes! Oh fuck, his orange eyes. My darling Mr. Biggie isn't a slutty rapist! What is wrong with him!?

She looked down between their bodies and bigfoot's emerging cock was covered with her blood.

Emily Thompson began screaming for help. For real this time.

CHAPTER 16

James Gallagher was just arriving back at the campsite after seeing the professor off when he heard the screaming.

(Even though the parking lot was only twenty minutes' walk away, it had taken James this long to return to camp because before Professor Marshall had driven off to town, he and his cousin had done some last minute planning concerning tomorrow's search, and that discussion had used up an hour of time.)

After taking a moment to determine it was Emily screaming and that the noise was coming from the ladies' tent, James transferred his flashlight to his left hand, then pulled out his gun and ran over there.

The tent's entrance flap had been ripped off and so even before he arrived there, James could see why his friend was yelling with all of her might. Sticking out of the tent were a pair of grossly oversized feet.

The fact that the giant feet currently lay at an angle to the ground surprised James, who at first thought someone was throttling Emily.

But then, playing the flashlight beam into the open tent revealed that bigfoot was ravishing her.

Bigfoot's here? As far as James could tell, bigfoot had entered the tent like he was crawling into a cave on his hands and knees, which had to be the sole reason the inflatable building still mostly existed.

Emily was almost invisible beneath the hairy giant, but each time the sasquatch lifted its huge body off of hers, James saw that Emily's thighs were completely bloody.

The sight of the blood and the noise Emily was making prevented James from becoming entranced by the realization that bigfoot was real, and he was finally having his long desired encounter with the elusive creature.

Where the hell have Jason and Amelia gotten to? James wondered angrily as he slipped past the giant feet and into the tent. *This needs to be documented, but I've gotta save Emily first.*

An even more puzzling question than Jason and Amelia's non-availability, James suddenly realized, concerned why their scanners and sensors—all that super-expensive cutting-edge tracking gear specifically designed to detect a hominid cryptid's approach—had failed.

Or, did we forget to activate the master unit? Emily and I—everyone was so tired and drunk that . . . Shit! I'll figure that out later!

Now that James was also inside the tent, crouched down and staring at the interspecies copulation, he was faced with a dilemma. He had to help Emily, and yet he knew he mustn't kill bigfoot—the creature was too precious to science. What he was now witnessing, and the current opportunity to record it on film, might not present itself again for the next hundred years.

But our damn crackhead cameraman is nowhere to be found. Nor is our pothead psychic! Those two jokers have likely wandered off somewhere to get stoned together!

That the pair weren't currently anywhere near the camp was obvious. Emily was making such a racket that everyone for a mile around must have heard her.

Bigfoot clearly hadn't heard James enter the tent, because he was still screwing away. Maybe Emily had noticed James come in, because her screams had now reduced to moans that were interspersed by the wet smacking together of their bodies. Emily's body was flopping up and down like she was skewered on bigfoot's cock and the hominid creature gave no indication of either stopping or slowing down his rutting.

I'll just shoot it in the ass, James decided. *That won't kill the thing!*

So James did that. He shot bigfoot in the left buttock. The noise of the gunshot filled the tent. Bigfoot gave a howl of agony.

And then, as if suddenly aware of the presence of a spectator to his sexual activity, the sasquatch climbed off of Emily and got to his feet.

Bigfoot's straightening up was of course at first hindered by the human-planned dimensions of the tent, with the cryptid's rising body threatening to uproot the tent pegs once his head hit the tent ceiling, but this vertical stalemate didn't last long, because bigfoot finally clawed the tent roof into shreds of fabric that fell aside like orange peels.

Then both bigfoot and James were standing in the open air, beneath forest and moon, with the walls of the tent around them.

James had one good look at the bleeding gash between his friend's thighs and then bigfoot was on him, towering over him. The monster's gore-slicked penis was still erect and seemed as long as James's arm. The cock dripped blood. And for some reason, the sasquatch's eyes were huge and orange, and seemed to be glowing. Also, the claws on his hands and feet seemed grossly disproportionate to the size of the extremities they each resided on.

Worst of all, shooting bigfoot in the ass didn't appear to have done anything to the creature except anger it.

Bigfoot opened his mouth and growled at James. Staring up into bigfoot's mouth, James got a very good look at the creature's dentition. In just the same manner as the nails on his hands and feet seemed oddly carnivore-inclined, bigfoot's teeth also seemed unusually numerous and too pointy to be those of an omnivore.

James quailed before the furry giant but managed to keep his cool and plan in this surreal stalemate that could have been ripped from a John Carpenter movie. As a long-time tracker and survivalist, he'd faced lots of dangerous outdoors situations, including once needing to subdue a maddened grizzly bear after he'd run out of bullets. He tried to convince himself that this was simply one more such case in which courage and finesse would yield dividends.

Bullet must have hit a bone. I'd better shoot him again . . . in the foot, this time! Then we'll have a blood trail to follow if he escapes.

But before James could get a shot off, bigfoot swatted the gun out of his hand. Almost like time had slowed down for his benefit, James watched the gun fly lazily through the air and hit the shredded canvas wall behind Emily.

James glanced at Emily. *She's still alive, but just barely. I need to get her to a hospital ASAP . . . but . . .*

But he had dire straits of his own to contend with. Because, bigfoot had just lifted him up off his feet. The creature had him under the shoulders and moved him as easily as if he were made of cardboard.

"Put me the fuck down!" James growled as bigfoot lifted him overhead. His mind had already shifted to survival mode and he began kicking at bigfoot. And even though he'd lost his gun, he still had his flashlight; and now he shone this in bigfoot's eyes, seeking to disorient the creature so it would drop him.

Oh, my dear God! James wondered, when he got a close-up look at the creature's face as it tried to blink away the flashlight beam. *Why the fuck are his eyes so goddam orange!*

Bigfoot clearly didn't take kindly to being kicked and having a light shone in his eyes, though James wasn't even sure exactly where he'd been kicking the beasty thing.

All of a sudden, James Gallagher became aware of a shearing pain in his back. A second later, similar stabbing pains hit James in the chest. Then, he heard the sound and simultaneously felt the agony of cracking bones.

What!? WHAT!!!???

Desperate now, James shone the flashlight on his own body. He was unable to see what felt like saw blades tearing into his back, but the front view was sufficient to completely horrify him. And he had good reason to be horrified: bigfoot had dug both of his thumbs into James's chest. Each monster digit was buried—beyond James's now-cracked ribs—deep in his flesh, up to the second knuckle, which meant their ends—and their claws—were now deep inside James's lungs; a fact confirmed a moment later when James spat out a mouthful of blood.

"Stop! I'm your friend!" James sputtered miserably at bigfoot, totally unable to comprehend what had driven such a reputedly quiet being to such heights of violence.

Maybe his sexual assault on Emily could be explained by saying he's sexually frustrated, but this kind of violence . . . Okay, I did shoot him first, James thought, with tears running down his face, because bigfoot had suddenly dug his claws even deeper into James's chest and had begun pulling them in opposite directions. *Yeah, shooting him in the ass like I did wasn't a friendly thing to do. Bad call that.*

And that was the last thought James Gallagher ever had. Because, with a sudden wrench, and a corresponding shower of blood, bigfoot pulled the left and right halves of James's torso completely apart. James head went with the left side—left arm, left lung and the heart, while most of his intestines went with his right side—the body's natural join continuing at his waist. It was a messy parting, and left bigfoot splattered in James's blood.

Once this violent act of separation was complete, Bigfoot dropped the dead man to the ground within the confines of the ruptured tent, where he lay like a human 'X'—two legs and two top halves.

Then bigfoot turned his attention back to Emily Thompson. His cock was still rock-hard, and had remained so all through his fight and disposal of the intrepid James Gallagher.

Emily was still alive too. She'd been holding out for rescue when James arrived in the tent, but now, after see the way bigfoot had killed her friend, she lost all hope of surviving.

She was right not to hope, because bigfoot hadn't yet had his orgasm; he was still horny as hell, and saw the bleeding and weeping human female on the floor as nothing more than a receptacle for his seed.

The now drug-enraged and monstrous creature, its mind swirling crazily in the throes of its Agent Orange addiction, knelt over Emily again, parted her legs, and resumed fucking her to death, this time with much more savagery than before.

CHAPTER 17

Bonnie B. Wilde admitted that it had to happen, given that she'd escaped in the middle of the night, and without a flashlight to guide her. After a while of trying to find her way down the mountain though the trees, she accepted that she was lost.

She felt furious with herself for getting lost, but also accepted that it wasn't really her fault. Although in theory a straightforward descent into the river valley below should be an easy thing to accomplish (all you had to do was keep going downwards along the slope of the mountainside, right?) in reality it had turned out to be a lot more complicated.

Bonnie had forgotten how ridged with cliffs and terraces this part of the mountain was, and so, more than once, after pushing her way out between a tangle of tree leaves, she had found herself standing right at the edge of a cliff with a precipitous drop; and then had had to backtrack and attempt to find another way downhill.

Her worry was that, assuming her sense of time was correct, she'd been making these sorts of back and forth trips for over an hour now, and sooner or later bigfoot might recover from his dizzy spell (or whatever he'd been suffering from earlier) and come hunting for her.

And to Bonnie B.'s mind, being recaptured by bigfoot would be a fate worse than death for her. She knew if that happened, she would never, ever see the outside world again.

But getting off the mountain was such hard going. And it was made worse for her by the fact that, in her rush to get away, she'd not bothered to pick up her sneakers.

So here I am, butt-naked and barefoot, and without a flashlight to light my way. It's no wonder I'm completely lost now. What's even more amazing is that I've not stumbled into a hole and broken both of my legs; or even worse, my back.

The half-moon hung in the sky and was bright enough to see by, but it kept being obscured by clouds and leaving Bonnie in the grip of a dread formless darkness in which the shadows kept taking on horrifying shapes.

She was walking carefully along what seemed a well-trodden forest trail, though she quickly realized she might be mistaken as she saw no reason folks would come hiking this high up on a regular basis. It was still too close to midnight to see clearly, but at least at this level of the hillside, the trees seemed to have a regular spacing on either side of her that suggested this was some kind of thoroughfare.

And this was how she came to the campsite.

Bonnie heaved an instant sigh of relief on seeing the pair of tents, and thanked her lucky stars. Then she hurried over towards the tents.

"Hey, I need help . . ." Bonnie began saying, but then an instinctive caution made her lower her voice. Something about this camp she'd stumbled into seemed wrong. She couldn't immediately tell what the matter was here, but something felt off to her.

Don't be an idiot. This is the middle of the night—possibly 1 a.m. in the morning. Everyone's fast asleep. I have to call out to wake them.

But then she realized what the problem was. The entrance flap of the nearer tent was wide open, and the tent itself seemed violently deformed.

No, the doorway isn't open, Bonnie realized. *Its flap has been ripped away, along with half of the right tent wall, and the tent roof has also been shredded and piled over on the wall. And there's a flashlight lying on the floor in there!*

Confused by what she was seeing, but knowing she needed help, Bonnie gathered her courage and walked across the clearing to investigate, almost stubbing her toe on a large rock as she skirted the burnt out campfire. Finally, she reached the opened-up tent and peered inside.

At first, Bonnie couldn't make proper sense of what she was looking at. The reason for this was because the flashlight on the floor of the tent was angled in such a way that as she approached the tent, its beam shone directly in her eyes. Her heart thudded with fear because she could hear loud slurping noises behind the flashlight, but couldn't see what was making them. She could just make out the outline of a hulking shape bent over inside there.

That sounds like a wild pig or something in there. Or maybe it's a bear ransacking the tent and looking for food because the campers are off somewhere.

The possibility of what was inside the tent being bigfoot never occurred to Bonnie because it was so low in height, and besides she'd left bigfoot whimpering in pain back in his cave, hadn't she? But Bonnie B. Wilde had overlooked the fact that that had been over an hour and a half ago, the interval since which she'd spent getting lost in the woods.

So Bonnie reached out a hand and picked up the flashlight, then she turned it around and played it properly on whatever was lurking inside there.

Then she froze in her tracks and all the blood drained from her face. She felt like an icicle. Fuck, no! Oh, my dear God, no!

There were two corpses inside the destroyed tent; a man who had somehow been ripped up into an X-shape, and a woman. The woman hadn't been ripped in two, but bigfoot was *eating* the woman. In the flashlight beam, the sasquatch's claws dripped red with the dead woman's blood, and shreds of her viscera and pieces of her flesh hung from its now-oversized teeth. Her entire belly was a gaping hole.

Bigfoot's hair was plastered with clotted blood. He looked like a nightmare; and his eyes—those horrible orange eyes whose origin Bonnie found impossible to understand . . .

Bonnie stood there, horrified, unable to move the flashlight beam away from bigfoot's face, and also unable to flee, which her mind was trying to tell her body to do.

But what the hell happened to him? He used to be so nice, so gentle. He always treated me really good. What could have possibly turned him into something like this?

But Bonnie now realized she had no time to wonder about the change in him. Seemingly irritated by the light she was playing into his eyes, bigfoot suddenly lurched to his feet, his head rising well above what remained of the tent walls.

Bonnie's fear paralysis left her the moment she saw that bigfoot had an erection, and that his huge and hard penis was coated in blood, blood that could only have come from the dead woman. And, in the brief moment after this when she and her former captor made eye contact, she could tell that this wasn't the same lovable creature that had abducted her; she understood that this monster now facing her intended to do to her exactly what he'd done to the dead woman, that is, fuck her to death and then feast on her.

Oh hell, no! That isn't gonna happen to me!

Bonnie turned and, not caring in what direction she went, began running away. At first she heard bigfoot coming after her, but then heard his grunt of frustration and a loud crash.

Perplexed by this, she halted her flight and turned around to see what had happened, shining her appropriated flashlight over the nearer tent. She felt relieved on seeing that bigfoot had somehow knocked over the front portion of the tent remnants and had gotten entangled up in a mess of fabric, beams, and guy ropes.

Realizing fate had granted her a second reprieve from the cryptid creature, Bonnie B. Wilde took to her heels. Any direction would do, so long as it took her away from here.

***

Of course Bonnie had no idea that the campsite she'd just left had been erected on the exact site where bigfoot had abducted her, or that in her blind panic, she'd taken off running in the exact same direction as her boyfriend Donnie had when he'd been following after the pair of them.

And so, just as it had been to Donnie, it was a great surprise to Bonnie, when she slipped at the exact same place where Donnie had, and then vanished from sight also.

Her disappearance wasn't a magic trick. Unfortunately for Bonnie, the point at which she'd lost her footing was the beginning of a long sideways trench that extended outwards to a steep cliff, but which along the way, also fed the concealed entrance of another subterranean cave, a cave which had no other exit other than its upper entrance. The aisle of rock that approached the cave had a vertical twist in it, a vertical outcropping that shielded the cave entrance from exterior view, so that even from a helicopter one would have great difficulty finding it.

And so, once she fell into this cave, Bonnie B. Wilde was trapped for good.

But getting out wouldn't be of concern for much longer for Bonnie, because the long vertical drop of about thirty yards which she fell from the entrance of the cave to its bottom broke both her back and her neck, leaving her fully paralyzed and staring up at the inaccessible circle of light overhead.

Her flashlight had made the trip down the mountainside and into the cave with her. And by its illumination, and by craning her neck the little that her paralysis would allow, Bonnie saw that she wasn't alone down here; but that her boyfriend Donnie had preceded her here.

Donnie's corpse lay at right angles to her own shattered body, bloated and with worms spilling from its face; and with a horrible rictus grin caused by vanished lips. If anything, he looked much more horrible than the dead woman in that bastard bigfoot's cave.

"Great to see you, baby; now we can carry on our love affair!" Donnie's corpse-face seemed to be saying with welcoming enthusiasm.

Bonnie B. Wilde burst into tears, and wondered how long it would be before she died too and the worms feasted on her just like they'd done to Donnie.

But she knew it wouldn't be long at all. Completely paralyzed like she was now, this time there would be no escaping death.

CHAPTER 18

This Saturday morning, Gary Bentley had the early shift. So, after kissing his wife Charlotte goodbye for the morning, and stepping over the mob of hungry raccoons who'd come to their house for breakfast, Gary placed his lunch in his ranger truck, climbed in himself, and zoomed off, heading for the mountains.

Last night Gary hadn't slept well. He'd kept tossing and turning and kept dreaming of a hairy monster with huge glowing eyes and a lot of horrible snaggly teeth that was chasing him around in circles.

Now, as he drove to work Gary laughed over the crazy nightmare.

I just spooked myself out, that's all. There's nothing to worry about. Maybe I'm worried about bigfoot getting his hands on some Agent Orange. But that's ridiculous. For one thing, there's no such thing as bigfoot. Everyone except Ben Marshall knows that. And for another thing, even if bigfoot did exist, where the hell would he get Agent Orange from to eat? From what I hear, that stuff is hard to find even in town now, and Marshall isn't likely to go hiking with a group of hardcore crackheads!

In this amused frame of mind Gary motored past the main Sleepaway Campground sign and turnoff, and instead turned off the highway a mile farther up, onto the back road that led to the upper, and lesser visited Thorne Knob hiking trails.

The first thing Gary noticed on pulling into the parking lot which ended the access road, was that the parking lot was deserted.

Gary frowned. *That's odd. Marshall's white camper should be here at least.* Then he grinned. *Or have they already found bigfoot? Or maybe Marshall finally wised up that bigfoot's merely a figment of their fevered imaginations and everyone's headed home?*

Gary almost turned his truck around and drove off because of this very thought. But his more conscientious side prodded him to at least make a quick survey of the area. Clearly, nothing was amiss here, but he'd feel better if he made certain that was the case.

So he parked his pickup truck and climbed out. From what Professor Marshall had told him, his expedition would be setting up camp about two and a half miles from the parking lot, near where a second hiking trail that accessed yet higher up the mountain split off from the first.

The morning was nice and calm, exactly the way Gary liked it.

Oh yes, this is a glorious day; one I'm certain can only get better and better; exactly the sort of day when one knows all is well with the world. If Ben Marshall and his nerdy friends are still here, I'll just say a quick hello to them, maybe even share a cup of coffee with them; and then I'll head back down to make my postponed tour of those deserted hiking trails that head towards Lake Placid. That area's like a pit stop for litterers, 'cos us rangers hardly ever patrol over there.

Gary Bentley of course had no idea how wrong his perception of things was, or of the level of shit storm that was about to rain down on his unsuspecting head.

CHAPTER 19

Jason and Amelia were hurriedly getting dressed after a frenetic burst of early morning sex, when Jason stopped putting on his pants and looked around him.

"What's the matter, babe?" Amelia asked, on seeing the anxious look on his face as he turned out his pants pockets.

"I can't find my stash of crack," he replied her. "I was certain I had it on me last night."

"Ah, don't worry about it," Amelia said, hugging him closely. "You most likely forgot it at camp, before we set out for here." She felt very warm and loved after their lovemaking and was pleased that Jason seemed to want to continue to be with her. She had a really good feeling about their future; and yet also had the feeling that if care wasn't taken in the immediate future, their relationship might be a very short one.

In fact, Amelia Blackwood had a confused feeling about this morning. Danger lurked somewhere nearby, she felt; and really terrible danger at that. But of the specific nature of the danger, she couldn't be certain.

Jason nodded, but looked confused. "Yeah, I guess I did, but I could've sworn I had it on me." He frowned at Amelia. "I don't want to seem dependent on crack while I'm around you, baby, but I'll be in a lot of trouble if I have to go without it for the rest of our stay here. I'm even shocked I made it all the way through the night without having to fix myself."

Amelia nodded that she understood. "Maybe us smoking pot helped." Amelia, who had suddenly remembered that she'd flung Jason's precious crack away while under the influence of said marijuana, now sought to distract her lover. "Man, the professor's gonna have our asses for breakfast if he gets back to camp before us."

Jason nodded. "I can't believe we both left Emily alone. That was really selfish of us both."

Emily shook her head. "Not really. She has James to look after her. Maybe she'll even seduce him into bed."

Jason laughed at that. "Emily seduce James? Not on this planet. You know what? I think Emily is in love with bigfoot."

Amelia, who was relieved that for the time being Jason had forgotten about the missing drugs, nodded. "Yeah, I know. There's this creepy way she keeps personalizing her references to him, calling him Mr. Biggie, as if they're bosom friends. Hey, what's that?"

Jason had been peering down into the grass. He straightened up again, holding up two small orange nuggets, which Amelia realized must have spilled from the pack she'd thrown away.

He looked perplexed however. "These'll have to do for now," he finally said, throwing the candy-like things into his mouth.

"You're chewing it like gum," Amelia said, feeling disturbed at the sight. "Aren't you supposed to like *smoke* crack—like with a crack pipe?"

Jason shook his head. "Not this sort." Once he'd swallowed the cocaine chunks, he nodded at her. "Come on, we'd better get back to camp fast, before the boss arrives and chews us out."

They set off in a hurry.

***

After Amelia and Jason had both been walking for a while, and yet seeming not to get any closer to their destination, Jason suddenly halted their progress with a hand on Amelia's arm.

"What?" she asked.

"Shush!" Jason whispered in an insistent voice, and pulled her back through the leaves. "Don't move a muscle!"

Amelia froze, suddenly aware of danger nearby; once more a danger she couldn't identify. But then she gasped and almost shrieked out, as a giant hairy creature lumbered into view and walked towards them, barely ten feet away. The monster being (which seemed to be about eight or nine feet tall) was partly obscured by leaves and brush, but there was no mistaking what species it was.

"That's bigfoot!" Amelia whispered in excitement. But it was a scared excitement. "But bigfoot is supposed to be a gentle creature," Amelia said. "He's covered in blood. Why the hell is he covered in blood?"

"We don't want to find out," Jason said. "We just wanna wait here quietly and not attract the big guy's attention."

Amelia silently agreed with Jason. They couldn't see bigfoot's face, but when the giant creature raised his right hand and pushed a branch aside, they saw that his hand was coated in blood and left dark red smears on the greenery it pushed through.

Along with the intense musky animal reek and nasty smell of spilled blood that hit them when bigfoot paused in his progress and sniffed the wind, Amelia also sensed an almost overpowering psychic reek of death coming towards them from the giant creature. But luckily, they were able to smell bigfoot the way they could because they were standing downwind of the creature, which apparently hindered him from smelling them too.

And also, because most of bigfoot's face was hidden by leaves, he clearly couldn't notice them watching him. But when his mouth momentarily came into view, Amelia cringed at the sight of his bloodstained chin and lips; and of his teeth, which had scraps of flesh and skin caught between them.

Amelia became aware that Jason had his cellphone out and was making a video of bigfoot. He continued filming until bigfoot resumed his motion away from them.

"Well, at least now we've concrete proof that this particular cryptid isn't a myth," Jason said with satisfaction, and then put his phone away again.

"I don't know about you," Amelia said, "but that's not the bigfoot I expected to find here in these woods. That creature that just walked away from us is a murderous monster."

She turned and looked intently into Jason's face. "Listen, babe, something is really wrong here. We need to hurry to our camp and warn the others that we're all in grave danger. Did you see bigfoot's face? His expression was completely soulless. Bigfoot is now completely evil."

Now she and Jason really hurried back to their camp.

CHAPTER 20

While Amelia and Jason were hurrying back to the campsite, Gary Bentley had already arrived there and was staring in horror at the two dead bodies.

Gary had already thrown up and was now simply staring in horror, gun in hand, momentarily confused as to what to do next, because as expected, neither his cellphone nor walkie-talkie was in receiving distance of a signal, and he couldn't call the ranger station or the police for assistance.

Oh my God, what happened here!

Gary's first impression was that a crazed grizzly bear was responsible for the massacre he was looking at.

The woman's corpse had been savaged beyond belief, her flesh scattered in chunks all over the tent enclosure, which itself remained in name only now, and consisted merely of flaps of tent material shredded in pieces.

But even if it's considerable that a bear killed this woman, what happened to James? He's been pulled apart from neck to waist. Even if a bear had the strength to accomplish something like this—and I really doubt that it could—it would also need a pair of hands.

Gary felt nauseated again and steadied himself. Then, he staggered over to a tree stump positioned by the long-extinguished campfire and sat on it.

Where the hell are the others? None of them are in the other tent.

Visions of another massacre filled his head. *But those other two previous animal massacres were triggered by Agent Orange, and I assume that's out of the picture here.*

"Hey, Ranger! Ranger, what's going on here?"

Gary looked up in relief on hearing Professor Marshall's voice. At least the professor wasn't dead.

Shaking his head, Gary arose from the tree stump, holstered his firearm, and quickly walked over to block off the professor's view of the sight inside the destroyed tent. He didn't think the man would be able to stomach the sight of the corpses, particularly since he knew Professor Marshall was sweet on the Emily woman.

But apparently, Gary had moved too late and Professor Marshall had already gotten a good eyeful, because the professor began howling, "Oh, Emily! God, no! Oh my God!" Then, with tears in his eyes, he looked at Gary. "What the hell happened to her, man? What the hell did this to Emily?"

"Your cousin James is dead too," Gary said, stepping out of Marshall's way, so the man could see what he was talking about.

Professor Marshall took a good look at both corpses and threw up.

"I don't know what the hell happened to them both," Gary explained as Marshall wiped his mouth clean with the rear of his hand. "I just got here and found them both this way. By the looks of things, they've both been dead for hours."

The two men regarded each other in silence. Professor Marshall kept on weeping, like the tears wouldn't ever stop.

"Bigfoot killed them both," Amelia's voice said nearby.

Both men looked around at she and Jason. Professor Marshall removed his glasses and dried his eyes.

"Bigfoot killed Emily and James," Amelia said again.

Gary shook his head at Amelia. "Now, let's get something straight, lady. This is no time for crappy jokes. I've got two dead people here who're friends of yours, so please show them some respect. You and I both know that there's no such thing as bigfoot. Grow up, wilya? You're long out of kindergarten!"

But Jason also shook his head. "I think she's right; bigfoot killed them."

Gary had had enough of the pair. "I don't know what the two of you have both been smoking, but take your stoned asses away from me before I kick 'em both down the mountain!"

While making this angry tirade, Gary Bentley was aware that there was something oddly familiar about the man he was addressing. And no, it wasn't that he was a television personality. Aside from his celebrity, there was something else about him that hovered right on the edge of Gary's mind, but which he found himself unable to place his finger on.

Instead, he stared angrily at Benjamin Marshall. "Hey, man, they're your people. You talk some sense into them."

The professor nodded. "Yes, alright, let me handle this." Then he looked sternly at Jason and Amelia and gestured to the struck-down tent. "Please both of you stop making light of this. Emily and James are both dead in there."

"We know," Amelia said. "And we're telling you that bigfoot killed them both."

Gary had now had enough. "And where were the two of you when this happened?" he asked in a no-nonsense voice. "You two are starting to sound like a pair of perpetuators holding onto the flimsiest alibi in criminal history."

In response to Gary's question, Jason thrust his cellphone at the man. "We're not joking, ranger. We just ran into bigfoot on our way back here. Here, see for yourself."

Gary hedged and shook his head at the proffered cellphone. "I've no desire to be drafted into you people's airheaded fantasies."

But Jason's statement had caught the professor's attention. "Let me see that," he said, taking the cellphone from Jason's hands. Then after a few seconds of watching the video Jason had already loaded up onscreen, Marshall tapped Gary on the shoulder, and said in shocked voice. "Ranger, I think you'd better get a load of this."

Gary reluctantly watched the video too, and then in a shocked voice, he asked Jason and Amelia, "Where the hell did you say you recorded this?"

"About a mile north of here," Amelia replied. "We were walking back from . . . it doesn't matter . . . and then suddenly there was bigfoot right in front of us."

"He was fucking covered in blood and seemed crazy," Jason added. "Once he'd left, we headed back here as fast as we could."

Gary was convinced now. It was either Marshall's team had hired the guys who did the Marvel Studio's special effects to fake this film for them, or he'd just watched the real thing. The fact that he had two dead bodies to deal with in the here and now, only served as concrete proof that he'd not just watched a faked video, but that bigfoot was real.

"What the hell are we gonna do now?" Amelia asked, after having peeked at the bodies corralled in the tent enclosure and managing not to puke her guts out, like Jason was doing beside her.

"We play it safe and get the hell away from here, before bigfoot returns to kill us all," Gary said. "None of our cellphones will work up here and neither does my walkie-talkie. So I suggest that we hurry as fast as we can down to our vehicles and get the hell out of Dodge, and leave this mess for the professionals to handle."

"In this case, we were supposed to be the professionals," Professor Marshall said sadly. "But I guess you're right." Then he addressed Jason. "I noticed James's gun somewhere near Emily's body. Please retrieve it. We might need it."

Jason looked like he might puke again at the request, so Gary hurriedly fetched the gun from beside Emily's body.

Gary handed the retrieved gun to Jason. This was followed by a brief pause while the cryptid hunters each collected some important possessions of theirs.

Then, with both Gary and Jason holding their firearms at the ready, their small group hurried down the mountain trail towards the parking lot and safety. Aware of the danger that might be stalking them already, they first jogged and then ran down the hillside.

And all through that rush to the parking lot, Gary kept on thinking that there was something quite wrong about Professor Marshall's friend Jason, but for the life of him, just right now he couldn't put his finger on what that something was.

CHAPTER 21

By now bigfoot was in a crazed state, having spent half of the night wandering aimlessly. The huge creature was tormented by violent visions of himself rending flesh and devouring it, killing and fucking, a primal, orange-tinted vision of hell that he had no hope of understanding.

Now that the day had dawned, both the insanity in bigfoot's head and the wracking pain in his massive body seemed to increase to a point where he walked holding his head. He was of course unaware that he was suffering withdrawal symptoms from the drug named Agent Orange and that the only way to make those symptoms go away was to consume more of the drug.

He did know one thing, however; that there was a large amount of that orange substance he'd consumed last night very close by, and he needed to have it fast. His junkie instinct demanded that he find the Agent Orange as quickly as he could and eat it all.

Bigfoot had always had a great sense of smell. But now, that sense was quadruple-amplified, and it was pointing him unerringly towards the parking lot that the three humans were fleeing towards.

In a burst of desperation, less the fleeing humans reach the precious orange substance before he did and eat it all up, leaving none for him, bigfoot began charging through the trees to cut them off.

And since he wasn't following the hiking trail, he soon overtook the humans who were desperate to avoid him.

CHAPTER 22

It was a crazy breakneck run down to the parking lot. And yet, when they reached there, they saw that bigfoot had arrived there before them.

"Shit!" Gary Bentley said when they saw bigfoot shambling towards the parked camper and ranger pickup truck.

After quickly ducking back into concealment behind the bushes that bordered the parking lot, everyone peeked out to watch bigfoot. Amelia began softly chanting a mantra, while Jason aimed his video camera at bigfoot and began recording him.

"How the hell are we going to get away now?" Professor Marshall asked in a worried voice, "the damn thing is heading for our vehicles."

Yes, this was true. Bigfoot had emerged from the woods and entered the parking lot on the opposite side of the two vehicles from the humans. The sasquatch, which was holding its head between both hands like it hurt, was now maybe five yards away from Gary's pickup truck, which was parked on the far side of Professor Marshall's white RV.

At this distance, bigfoot's eyes seemed reddish to ranger Gary Bentley, but he quickly dismissed their unnatural coloration as resulting from the amount of blood the creature was covered with. Or, maybe bigfoot naturally had bloodshot eyes—who could say, seeing as nobody had ever gotten a good picture of the cryptid?

But really, it was simply that Gary Bentley subconsciously desired to ignore the obvious, not wanting to accept that such Agent-Orange-related disasters could really occur in threes, and on his turf . . . again. This too, was the reason he'd not instantly made the connection between the color of the cameraman's eyes and Agent Orange.

"We'll never reach the camper before he reaches us," Gary said. "We need a plan."

He stared down at his walkie-talkie and cussed: "Damn how there's no cellphone reception at this height." Then he looked at the gun in his hand, and gestured over at Jason. "Hey, put the damn camera down, we need to shoot the—"

But then Gary stopped speaking and instead gaped in amazement, because right then, in a rage over something, bigfoot grasped the rear of Gary's pickup truck and flipped it right over. Almost like it was a full-scale papier-mâché model without any real weight, the ranger truck landed on its topside and then skidded fifty feet away, where it halted, still upside-down, and now slowly rotating.

Without paying any attention to the overturned vehicle, bigfoot walked on towards the professor's RV.

"I didn't think sasquatches were that strong," was all Professor Marshall could say. "I wonder what the guys back at the Bigfoot Field Researchers Organization will make of this when we tell them."

"Do you still think shooting it's a good idea?" Jason asked Gary. "We may just make it mad."

Gary considered his own firearm again. "You're making a great point," he then agreed.

"So what do we do now?" Amelia asked in fright. "You guys all saw what bigfoot did to Emily and James. If it gets hold of us too, we're screwed."

Meanwhile bigfoot had reached their RV, and for the moment at least, was circling it, while also peering at it with interest, like he was trying to make up his mind about something. This near to them, they could see how bloody the massive sasquatch's body really was, all the way to his flaccid genitalia. Just like when Amelia and Jason had earlier encountered the sasquatch, strips of meat that had gotten stuck between bigfoot's teeth still dangled from his mouth.

Jason said, "I dunno why, but he's looking at our camper like a toddler trying to figure out how to open up a sardine can."

"This stalemate isn't gonna last forever," Professor Marshall said.

"No, it ain't," Gary readily agreed. "We need a distraction of some kind, before that big bloodstained monster over there loses whatever fascination he has with the camper and heads for us again. And like our cameraman has already pointed out, our guns don't look to be much help against bigfoot."

"What have you got in mind?" Amelia asked, as almost on cue, bigfoot stopped looking at the RV and stared their way. But then, he once more turned his attention back to the vehicle.

"We need to distract it away from the RV, so we climb in and drive off," Gary explained. "I'm gonna try to do that. Now listen, I'll head towards bigfoot and shoot at it, to get its attention. Once it turns to attack me, you guys all pile into the RV and drive over to me and pick me up."

"That's dangerous," the professor pointed out.

Gary shrugged. "We've no other options. Besides, I'm armed. I'll have some protection from its raging for a few minutes till you guys arrive with the vehicle."

"I'll come with you, ranger," Amelia said, after a glance over at bigfoot, who was now peering inquisitively into the recreational vehicle's side windows.

Gary stared at her in surprise. "Oh no, ma'am. You just heard the professor. It's way too dangerous."

But Amelia shook her head. "I know, but I'll do it anyway." Waving a hand to silence Gary's next protest, she explained: "Listen, remember that from what we saw at the campsite, bigfoot raped Emily to death . . ."

"Oh, please, don't remind me," Professor Marshall said miserably.

". . . What I'm getting at is, we know he's attracted to human women. Before attacking Emily, he also abducted Bonnie B. Wilde. So if—"

"Pardon me," Gary interrupted, "but who's Bonnie B. Wilde?"

"A YouTube celebrity," Professional Marshall explained. "She went missing up on this very mountain. She's largely the reason why we came here."

"Okay, I get that," Gary said, then looked at Amelia again. "Please go on, ma'am."

Amelia went on: "So, what I'm saying is, seeing as we now know that bigfoot likes human women . . . if I'm with you, ranger, there's a higher chance of bigfoot leaving the camper to come after us, which gives us a better chance of escaping."

"Okay," Gary grudgingly agreed. "But stay safe behind me."

Professor Marshall grudgingly nodded too, then looked at Jason. "It only needs one of us to get the camper. The other one should be with the others—more firepower in case of trouble."

Jason handed the professor his gun and camera. "You go with them. I'm a better driver than you."

Marshall looked suspiciously at the gun and then took it from Jason and handed him the keys to the vehicle instead. "Alright, how do we do this?" he asked Gary.

"We three run diagonally across the car park," Gary told them. "Follow my lead, and stay very close to me. We wanna get close to bigfoot, but not so close that he can easily get to us. Once were at a good, safe distance, Amelia will call out to bigfoot, and we guys will get ready to shoot." He looked at Jason. "You stay concealed here until bigfoot has left the RV and is coming after us. Then you leap in, start it up and reverse. If possible, ram into bigfoot while you're reversing and knock him down. Then you circle around him and pick us up. Got it?"

"Loud and clear," Jason agreed.

"Alright, let's do this," Gary said. "'Cos bigfoot seems to be about to pull your camper apart too, which'll mean the end of our ride out of here, and likely our four deaths at his bloody hands."

CHAPTER 23

As planned, Gary, Amelia, and Professor Marshall set off across the parking lot.

"Bigfoot is paying no attention at all to us," Amelia said as they padded softly over the gravel. "It seems like it would be so easy to simply keep on going, to leave the parking lot and head down the mountain before it notices us."

"Don't count on it," Gary said. "I don't know what's in your ride that interests the sasquatch so much, but . . ."

"But . . . we'd better distract it fast," Professor Marshall said worriedly. "It's starting to wreck the RV."

This was accurate. In a spray of glass, Bigfoot had just punched a hole through the offside windscreen.

"Okay, let's do this!" Gary told the others.

"Hey, bigfoot," Amelia screamed out. "I'm here waiting for you!"

At the sound of her voice, the sasquatch, who'd been fiddling inside the shattered camper window, froze for a moment. He turned towards them and growled and spat, and for the first time Gary Bentley got a proper (and undeniable) look at the color of his eyes.

Oh no, you gotta be shitting me! Gary thought in horror. *Not again. Dear, sweet Jesus, please not again. But how in the hell . . . up here of all places?*

But bigfoot was already turning his attention away from them and back to the RV again.

"Keep calling out to him," Professor Marshall told Amelia. "Just continue."

"Hey, Mr. Biggie!" Amelia yelled. "I'm waiting for you. Don't you want me just the way you wanted Emily?"

"I wish you'd stop mentioning Emily," Professor Marshall groaned to himself.

But it had worked. Amelia had once more gotten the raging sasquatch's attention. This time bigfoot had pulled his hand out of the shattered window and was staring at her with interest.

Amelia strode a few steps forward, until Gary called out, "Ma'am, please stop, that's far enough!"

So Amelia stopped moving and resumed speaking to bigfoot. "Hey, Mr. Biggie! I'm waiting for you! Come and get me!"

Then Amelia ripped her top open, exposing her breasts. She cupped her breasts at the sasquatch and squeezed them at him. "See, see, how much larger they are than Emily's? I'm certain you didn't even enjoy fucking her like you'll love fucking me."

Marshall was by now almost beside himself with barely suppressed rage. "For fuck's sake, stop mentioning Emily," he sputtered to himself.

"Hey, professor, it's working," Gary told him. "Bigfoot is heading our way. Get ready to shoot."

And it was true. Bigfoot was now headed their way. And if there was any doubt in anyone's minds as to why he was walking towards them, that doubt was wiped out when the sasquatch's penis began hardening.

"Oh, fuck," Ameila quailed in horror as the blood-splattered organ grew fully erect, "You're telling me that Emily had all of *that* inside of her?"

"Just keep seducing it," Gary told her. "Jason's making his move now, we'll soon be out of here."

"Yeah, sure," Amelia said over her shoulder, though her voice was less confident now. "Hey, Mr. Biggie, come and get me!" she cooed, as the distance between them narrowed to about twenty yards.

Behind bigfoot, Jason had gotten in the RV now, but seemed to be having some trouble starting it up.

"What's wrong with the damn vehicle now?" Professor Marshall groaned. "This isn't a damned movie! No need for suspense and dramatics!"

"Get ready to shoot!" Gary told him. "Wait for my signal and aim for bigfoot's chest and head."

"No, aim for his dick!" Amelia hissed.

Then her voice became all sweetness and cream again and she once again cooed at the sasquatch while holding her breasts seductively: "Oh, Mr. Biggie! See what I've got for you! All for you-uu!"

But something had changed, and the trigger for the change seemed to be the sound of the RV finally starting up. All of a sudden, bigfoot froze where he was, and next, with his penis visibly softening by the second, he turned around and charged over at the vehicle.

"Fuck, we need to stop him!" Gary said as bigfoot reached the recreational vehicle and grabbed a hold of its rear, which happened right when Jason had just begun to reverse out of parking. But apparently, Jason hadn't yet built up enough speed for the RV to be dangerous to bigfoot, and in a replay of what had happened to Gary's truck, bigfoot simply grabbed hold of the rear of the RV and flipped it over too. Once over on its side, the truck skidded sideways towards the hiking trail that had brought everyone here, finally coming to a halt near the entrance to the parking lot.

Bigfoot immediately turned his attention back to the people approaching him. Gary fired at the sasquatch, but as he'd expected, even though the bullets produced bloody holes in bigfoot's body, the wounds didn't slow the sasquatch down, but rather just seemed to anger him.

Gary quit firing. "Quick, let's get Jason out of the camper!"

They all ran towards the overturned RV. When they reached the vehicle, Professor Marshall turned to Gary. "Hey, man, you and Amelia get Jason out of the camper. I'll keep watch."

"Better I stand watch," Gary said.

But Professor Marshall simply gestured ahead with the gun in his hand. "I don't know where you shot the big hairy sonofabitch, but its slowed him down a little."

Gary paid closer attention and saw that it was true; bigfoot was walking slower than previously. He still had those bugged-out demented orange eyes (which meant someone here had a lot of explaining to do) but he was slower than before.

He seemed angrier though.

"Just go, get Jason out of the camper!" Marshall insisted. "You may need to climb up on top of it, and I'm too out-of-shape to do that!" Professor Marshall grinned. "And besides, I wanna give this orange-eyed freako some payback for killing two members of my team."

Gary nodded and hurried around to the front of the RV, stopping beside the front tires, which of course now stuck out sideways. He'd had to do this sort of human retrieval once before, and the only sensible way into a vehicle that was lying on its side like this one was, was through the windshield.

Fortunately, in this case the windshield was already cracked and half out of place. Just as fortunately, Jason was alive and in one piece, and just needed some help to navigate his way through the windshield.

'Bang! Bang! Bang!' The noise took Gary's attention off of Jason and focused it back on bigfoot and Professor Marshall.

Bigfoot had just reached the professor. Most of the professor's shots must have missed their target, but one of bigfoot's ears was hanging off of the side of his head; the resulting wound was bleeding profusely.

But that was it for Professor Marshall, who seemed to have run out of bullets. With an enraged snarl, bigfoot swatted the professor to the ground and then stomped on his head. Marshall's head burst like a water balloon, with his brains squirting in all directions beneath the sasquatch's massive foot.

Gary looked away from the nauseating sight and in doing so, glanced back at Amelia and Jason. During the interval that he'd looked away from them, Amelia had continued pulling Jason out of the RV and so neither of them had witnessed the professor's gruesome death. But of course, there would be no avoiding their seeing his smeared corpse when they stepped out past the RV.

Jason finally wriggled his way out through the shattered windshield.

Gary heaved a sigh of relief. *Okay, now, we three had better make a run for it. But where the hell are we gonna head—?*

And that was when he realized that bigfoot was no longer in view on his side of the recreational vehicle.

Where the hell is he?

Then Amelia screamed in horror. Gary hurried around the front of the vehicle and saw that bigfoot had hold of Jason and was dragging him away.

"Shoot it! Shoot it!" Amelia was screaming with her top still popped open and her breasts bouncing fiercely as if to emphasize her terror.

Gary and Amelia both hurried forward to the rear of the van, where Gary raised his gun to shoot bigfoot, but bigfoot was holding Jason up in the air and so was making an unintentional shield out of him.

Then there was a sickening wrenching noise of flesh separating and suddenly Jason was in two complete halves. Bigfoot dropped both halves and then began fishing in one of them for something.

"What the hell is he doing?" Amelia whispered, as bigfoot searched the bloody corpse remains. Amelia had already looked to her left and had noticed Professor Marshall's corpse, with its head splattered as flat as a rug. As a result of this, her face was now white with terror, and she was so frightened that she'd forgotten how to scream. She was also clinging tightly to Gary, though if asked, she would insist she had no memory of grabbing hold of him.

Gary sighed. The mystery was finally explained when bigfoot fished out a large package from a trouser pocket on the right half of the corpse and began emptying the 'orange candy' it contained into his mouth.

"Fuck, so that's why the camper didn't immediately start up," he told his female companion. "Your cameraman boyfriend must have been retrieving the rest of his stash of Agent Orange from when he'd hidden it in the vehicle."

"Agent Orange? What the hell is that?" Amelia asked as they watched bigfoot greedily scarf the orange chunks down. The humongous creature was bleeding profusely from his gunshot wounds, and yet, as he ate the substance, Amelia could sense a terrible vitality surging through his body. Bigfoot was still far from dead, and what he was eating now was pure evil energy. "I found some on Jason last night, but didn't really understand what it was."

Gary could feel her body tremble against his and so wrapped a protective arm around her. "Ma'am, Agent Orange is a curse on society," he explained in a whisper. "It's one of the most potent and addictive drugs currently available. I'd been figuring there was something odd about your boyfriend ever since I first laid eyes on him, but I only just realized that his eyes had that faint orange tint to them like Agent Orange users sometimes get. Not as bad as that damn sasquatch though."

"I thought that was a normal side effect of crack usage," Amelia said.

"Not at all. But it's a side effect of Agent Orange for sure." Then Gary scratched his chin. "What I don't understand, however, is how the hell fucking bigfoot over there got his fucking oversized hands on an addictive quantity of the fucking drug. Was your dead boyfriend attempting to feed the animals or what?"

"Oh shit, that must be my fault," Amelia said, with tears now starting to stream down her face. "Last night, I threw Jason's stash away into the woods. Bigfoot must've found it and eaten it."

She really began weeping now. "Shit, I just got everyone killed."

"Come on, we'd best get the hell out of here right now," Gary said, gesturing over with his gun at bigfoot, who, after having consumed the Agent Orange, was now eating Jason's liver. "That damn sasquatch is hungry, but soon he'll be feeling horny again. And remember, you showed him your tits. He probably thinks you're waiting here now for him to come git ya and to show you his monster lovin'."

Amelia immediately pulled the separate sides of her top tightly around her body. "Yeah, of course, we should go. But why not just shoot it now, while it's feeding?"

Gary sighed. "Lady, I've got just two bullets left in this gun and no spares. If I miss hitting bigfoot somewhere deadly, we'll both be corpses very soon." He tugged Amelia after him. "Come along now. We can't outrun bigfoot, but I've a good idea of where we can ambush him and give ourselves a fighting chance of winning this conflict."

CHAPTER 24

"Gary hastily led the way back towards the camp.

"What if he can't find us?" Amelia enquired as the two of them jogged past the cryptid team's erstwhile camping site, with its gruesome landmark of a wrecked and blood-splattered tent. "Not that I'm that desirous that he comes calling, but . . . I'm certain you know what I mean."

"We don't need to worry 'bout that," Gary replied her. "Animals on Agent Orange can smell better than sharks in water. Oh, he'll get here alright, and very soon too."

Amelia nodded. They were about a hundred yards past the campsite now, and then Gary slowed to a fast walk, turned right, and led them off of the trail, past a large sign warning 'Danger; Steep Cliffs; Keep To Hiking Trail,' and on through the trees to a less wooded area, past a second warning sign, and then into an area of the forest that for some reason seemed oddly familiar to Amelia, though she couldn't have said why that was.

"We stop right here," Gary said suddenly. Now, we've gotta be really careful here, and I'll explain why."

"I'm listening," Amelia said, shivering and with her arms wrapped tightly around herself. "I still can't believe all this crap is happening to me . . . and all because of me."

Gary smirked. "Don't beat yourself up about it. You had no way of knowing what throwing those drugs away would set in motion. You probably imagined you were doing your boyfriend a favor by disposing of them."

"I did," Amelia admitted. "I thought he didn't need them anymore." Then she frowned. "But all of a sudden you seem very calm about all this, ranger. Almost blasé in fact."

Now Gary laughed. "Oh, I've been in this situation twice before. First time, it was a raccoon that got cracked up; a huge crocodile the second time."

"A crocodile . . . ?" Amelia began asking, but Gary shushed her. "No time to explain in detail. I think I hear bigfoot coming. We gotta set our plan in motion."

Amelia began shivering harder still. "Okay, okay, okay, what do I do now?"

Gary took her arm and steered her across the clearing, to a point where there were lots of high and intertwined bushes that almost formed a living latticework along the forest floor. "Stand right here and seduce him again, that's all," he said.

Amelia looked confused. "But, if I do that, he'll grab me and rape me. He'll rape me to death, like he did to Emily."

But Gary smiled and shook his head. "No, he won't. Just trust me. I ain't brought you back here just to watch you die."

Amelia nodded in confusion, but then stared suspiciously at Gary. "Where are you going to be during this time?"

"I'll be right behind you," Gary explained. "I'm aiming to get a clear shot at his head. I doubt sasquatches have nine lives like cats do. And anyway, so far this one has been very lucky, that both myself and Ben Marshall—God rest the good professor's soul—have missed hitting him anywhere critical. But a well-placed bullet to the brain will stop even an elephant."

"I'm trying to share your confidence," Amelia admitted as the sasquatch showed in the distance.

Amelia quailed. Bigfoot once more had his erection and a massive one it was, a fact made even more terrifying for the waiting woman by the fact that the giant tumescent penis was still covered with Emily's blood, even though that blood was now dried and caked.

Once bigfoot saw the two humans, he flung away the human hand he had been gnawing on and then roared at them like a lion, showing them the entirety of his altered dentition. By now his entire head was painted red with spilled blood. The only non-crimson portion of him above his shoulder were his two orange eyes.

"Just remember one thing!" Gary whispered harshly as bigfoot neared them. "Whatever else in the world you do right now, no matter how terrified you are, do not run forward! I repeat, do not run forward!"

"Please just shut up," Amelia pleaded. "I'm frightened enough as it is!"

Amelia parted the flaps of her top and began playacting again. "Ooh, bigfoot darling, ooh. Come to me, please. My pussy is aching for you, sopping wet just for you." She began squeezing her breasts again. "See these big juicy titties? Come here and fuck me right now, you big hairy loverboy. Give me all of your fantastic huge cock. Oh yummy, baby, I need it so much!"

Like it or not, Amelia's cooing was having the desired effect on bigfoot, who, with his glowing orange eyes focused on her bared breasts, hurried towards her, paying no attention whatsoever to the forest ranger who was standing right next to her and was aiming a gun at his head.

Bigfoot got closer and closer to Amelia, who began being scared that the forest ranger was actually crazy and that if she didn't run for her life right now, she was going to die here in the forest, killed and eaten by Bigfoot.

But right before she would have begun running for safety, Amelia felt a spiritual calm holding her in place.

No, the ranger wasn't lying, she realized. *I'm not in any danger, nothing bad is going to happen to me.*

And then, when bigfoot was about five yards away from her, and Amelia had begun reconsidering that maybe this strange psychic survival confidence she felt was really a long-repressed death wish, bigfoot suddenly growled in surprise and vanished from sight, slipping downwards and sideways through the latticed-up brush.

At first, Amelia could hear the sounds of the sasquatch's claws clutching for purchase at the ground, but suddenly that stopped and the only noise was that of a heavy body sliding rapidly away through grass; and then . . . silence.

It was only now that Amelia realized where she was standing:

This is the exact point where Bonnie B. Wilde's boyfriend Donnie vanished in that video. Soooo . . .

She looked at Gary in surprise and pointed at the tangle of foliage. "Is there a hole there?"

But he shook his head. "No, just a trench with a deceptively steep slope that leads to a drop over the cliff side of about two hundred feet." While explaining, Gary pointed outward from the mountain and then inwards again to a few feet ahead of Amelia's feet. "The trench didn't always used to be here, but I think a chunk of rock got dislodged and rolled downhill, leaving a sloping groove running along the ground. And, the brush here now grows inward on both sides of the trench and their tangle completely obscures the depression, like there's nothing amiss here."

"But this is really dangerous," Amelia said, noting that even after bigfoot's disappearance, the place he'd vanished through looked as undisturbed and innocuous as before she'd stood beside it. "You forest rangers should do something about it."

Gary nodded. "We did. First of all, we cleared the foliage away, so folks could see the danger for themselves, but it grows back remarkably fast and somehow always makes the same innocent-seeming tangle. That's why we've a number of signs posted on the trails to prevent campers from stepping out this far. But really, we plan to fence the area off. God knows who else could fall over the edge here."

"I think someone already did," Amelia said, remembering Donnie, but she didn't elaborate further.

Gary gestured to Amelia to carefully step away from where she was standing. Indeed, Amelia herself needed little prompting to be cautious.

"We're safe from bigfoot now," Gary told the woman.

"Are you sure of that?"

He nodded. "Yeah, with that many bullets in him, there's no way he's going to survive that high of a fall. The impact on the rocks down there is certain to do him in; they'll break every bone in his damn bloodthirsty body." Then Gary sighed. "In a way it's sad tho'. First time in history that anyone gets conclusive proof that bigfoot is real, and we go and kill him."

Then he extended his hand to Amelia. "Come on, let's head down the mountainside to where we can call for help."

CHAPTER 25

Down at the bottom of the hidden hillside cave, Bonnie B. Wilde was bemoaning her horrible fate.

Here I am, totally paralyzed from the neck down, without a damn help of saving myself, and still it's taking me forever to die.

Worst of all, Bonnie wished that her sense of smell was paralyzed too. She couldn't stop smelling Donnie, who reeked like a stall of rotting racehorses. And worse still, a good number of the worms and insects that had been feeding on his corpse had already begun investigating Bonnie's body too. Of course she couldn't feel them crawling over her, but she had sufficient neck motion to be able to see them do so, which was just as bad.

And she'd begun feeling very thirsty too.

She knew it was morning time again now. The faint sunlight streamed in through the upper vent of the cave, and it made her depressed.

If I could just die right now, Bonnie wished. *That would be a blessing.*

Her wish was about to be granted. For a brief moment the sunlight filtering through the overhead cave entrance was blotted out; and when daylight returned to the cave, Bonnie made out a massive hairy form falling down towards her.

Fuck, it's bigfoot! she thought in alarm in the two or three seconds before the blood-soaked sasquatch crashed down on top of her, completely crushing her to death.

That was it for Bonnie B. Wilde.

Bigfoot died too, his head shattering to pieces on a rock, cracking open like a coconut and spilling his brains everywhere, brains that had been turned bright orange in color by Agent Orange.

CHAPTER 26

Gary Bentley thought it was crazy, but it was the truth. Search hard as they could, neither the forest rangers nor the police could find any trace of bigfoot. For sure, there was an excess of the creature's trademark footprints everywhere, even some bloody ones, but no sign of the creature's corpse.

"Weren't for all these corpses everywhere, I might have imagined it all," Gary told his female companion (who, now that the crisis was over, had properly introduced herself as Amelia Blackwood).

Both of them were seated in the back of a police cruiser, waiting to be driven to the police station for an intense debriefing. Amelia, who'd changed her top before the calvary had arrived, nodded as they watched the coroner's van drive away with its load of corpses.

"No one's gonna believe us, right?" she asked Gary. "They'll say it was a crazy grizzly bear. But . . . but, Gary . . . Jason filmed it. No one can deny bigfoot's existence now."

Gary laughed. "Don't be naïve, Amelia," he replied the intense expression on her face. "This is the age when movie special effects often look more realistic than the real thing. Even if you uploaded the stuff Jason filmed to the internet, no one would take it seriously. They'd think it was simply more special effects."

"Yes, I get what you mean," Amelia said soberly. "It's ironic that everyone's been used to believing bigfoot's a myth for so long, we'll go on believing he doesn't exist, even if we met him face to face."

Gary laughed at that. "Very well put." He was relieved that he could still laugh, after all he'd just been through.

What would happen to Jason's bigfoot recordings? Gary was certain that by this evening at the latest, copies of the recordings would be on their way to Area 51 for detailed analysis.

And with the way damn bigfoot was doing all that killing, like he was a killing machine? Yeah, sooner or later one of our military's top brass is sure to suggest that the US Government find bigfoot ASAP and weaponize him.

The End.

ABOUT THE AUTHOR

Gary Lee Vincent was born in Clarksburg, West Virginia and is an accomplished author, musician, actor, producer, director and entrepreneur. In 2010, his horror novel *Darkened Hills* was selected as 2010 Book of the Year winner by *Foreword Reviews Magazine* and became the pilot novel for *DARKENED - THE WEST VIRGINIA VAMPIRE SERIES*, that encompasses the novels *Darkened Hills, Darkened Hollows, Darkened Waters, Darkened Souls, Darkened Minds* and *Darkened Destinies*.

He has also authored the bizarro thriller *Passageway,* a tribute to H.P. Lovecraft, *When the Bedposts Shake,* an erotic horror, *THE BLACK CIRCLE CHRONICLES,* a five-part mini-series that includes the books, *Prove Your Love, Strange New Powers, Night Wings, Sheep Amongst Wolves,* and *Lord of the Birds,* and the *CRACKIMALS* series of horror-comedies (featuring titles *Crackcoon, Crackodile,* and *Cracksquatch*) in association with Director Brad Twigg and screenwriter Todd Martin of Fuzzy Monkey Films, who is doing their film counterparts.

Gary co-authored the novel *Belly Timber* with John Russo, Solon Tsangaras, Dustin Kay and Ken Wallace, and co-authored the novel *Attack of the Melonheads* with Bob Gray and Solon Tsangaras.

As an actor, Gary has appeared in over a hundred feature films, including *Faded Memories, Midnight,* and *My Uncle John is a Zombie,* and multiple television series, including *House of Cards, Mindhunter, The Walking Dead,* and *Stranger Things.* You can also find Gary in the motion picture adaptation of *Crackcoon,* playing Jonathan, the forest ranger.

As a director, Gary got his directorial debut with *A Promise to Astrid.* He has also directed the films *Desk Clerk, Dispatched, Midnight, Godsend, Strange Friends,* and *Shoulder Down: Road to Redemption.*

OTHER GREAT TITLES FROM

Burning Bulb

PUBLISHING

WWW.BURNINGBULBPUBLISHING.COM

GARY LEE VINCENT

PASSAGEWAY

IMPOUND

GARY LEE VINCENT

GARY LEE VINCENT'S
DARKENED
THE WEST VIRGINIA VAMPIRE SERIES

DARKENED WATERS

When the world goes to hell, the chosen must arise!

As Talman Cane orchestrates a flood of epic proportions in this third installment of the *Darkened* series the towns of Melas and Tarklin are caught completely off guard by the deluge. Hell-bent on finishing what they started, the evil brothers return to the lunatic asylum to take care of the witnesses and add to the ever-growing army of the undead.

Aided by Lucifer himself and the insane vampire demon Legion, the stage is set to channel all of the forces of hell to come forth. In an all-out race to survive, Jonathan, William, and Amanda soon discover they are up against impossible odds as Lucifer opens the Gateway to Hell, ushering in the zombie apocalypse and the End Times.

Find out who will survive this cosmic battle of the ages in *Darkened Waters!*

DARKENED SOULS

Melas and the Madison House are about to be rebuilt.
True evil is about to be reborne!

Young ex-priest and vampire-killer William is drawn back to the West Virginian town that almost killed him, where his vampire arch-enemy Victor Rothenstein still stalks the earth.

The town of Melas lies destroyed after the battle of the End of Days. But why is wealthy Jackie Nixon so eager to rebuild it using the bone dust of murdered souls?

Terrible evil has visited before, but the Gateway to Hell is about to be reopened in a horrific climax. And this time – it's personal.

WWW.DARKENEDHILLS.COM

Burning Bulb

GARY LEE VINCENT'S
DARKENED
THE WEST VIRGINIA VAMPIRE SERIES

DARKENED MINDS

Jackie Nixon intends to become Vampire Queen, but at what blood-drenched cost?

In this continuation to the explosive infernal saga begun in Darkened Souls, newly-turned vampire Jackie Nixon is taking no prisoners. Accompanied by her daughter, Kate, and by the captive vampire lord Victor Rothenstein, Jackie Nixon explores the Darkness. There, she intends to rouse the slumbering vampire race, bound under an ancient curse, and with their help, rule the human world.

But there's a deadly threat to Jackie's plans. Not just William who is trying to stop her, but her own royal ambitions. If Jackie performs the ritual to wake the sleeping vampires the wrong way, she could instead free the Red Beast of Hell, an unspeakable evil that even the undead fear.

DARKENED DESTINIES

With over 45 people missing after Jackie Nixon's party, the mysteries surrounding Melas and the Madison House keep getting darker.

Now, with legions of vampires at her command, can anything or anyone stop her from gaining complete control over all mankind?

The final battle has begun! As the Vampire Queen ascends her throne and sets to unleash the full forces of darkness, the fate of all things good hangs in the balance.

Burning Bulb
PUBLISHING

WWW.DARKENEDHILLS.COM

WHEN THE BEDPOSTS SHAKE

An Erotic Terror

GARY LEE VINCENT

STRANGE FRIENDS

GARY LEE VINCENT

PROVE YOUR LOVE

GARY LEE VINCENT

STRANGE NEW
POWERS

THE BLACK CIRCLE CHRONICLES - BOOK 2

GARY LEE VINCENT

NIGHT WINGS

THE BLACK CIRCLE CHRONICLES - BOOK 3

GARY LEE VINCENT

SHEEP AMONGST
WOLVES

THE BLACK CIRCLE CHRONICLES - BOOK 4

GARY LEE VINCENT

LORD OF THE
BIRDS
THE BLACK CIRCLE CHRONICLES - BOOK 5
GARY LEE VINCENT

From the Creator of DARKENED HILLS...

RIVER
A VAMPIRE'S NIGHTMARE

GARY LEE VINCENT

A Vampire's Nightmare Continues . . .

RIVER

Book 2 Icarus

GARY LEE VINCENT

THE BLIND MELODY

GARY LEE VINCENT

JEROME

A GHOST STORY

GARY LEE VINCENT